MY HEART BEATS FOR AN ATLANTA BOSS 2

D. NIKA

Copyright © 2018 by D. Nika

All rights reserved.

No part of this book may be reproduced in any form or by any electronic or mechanical means, including information storage and retrieval systems, without written permission from the author, except for the use of brief quotations in a book review.

❀ Created with Vellum

K.C. Mills Presents
My Heart Beats for an Atlanta Boss 2
By: D. Nika

ACKNOWLEDGMENTS

My Heart is pounding ya'll. My 6th book, I can't believe it!!

Let me first give all praises to the man above, without God none of this would be possible.

To my two babies Travon (Trae) and Trinity LaMya, I love y'all with everything I have in me and I do this for you both. Ya'll make me proud every day and I hope mommy is making you guys just as proud.

To my AMAZING husband John, thank you, babe, for believing in me and pushing me to go for my dreams. You have been encouraging me for years to write a book and I thank you. I love you Zaddy. (I still ain't got that MacBook)

To my parents, thank you both for believing in me and pushing me to continue when I wanted to give up.

To my daddy Darrell Robinson... RIP daddy, I hope you

looking down from heaven smiling and proud of me. I miss you so much. Gone but never ever forgotten!!!!

To my bestie/sister Monique, you already know what it is. I love you babe

To my big cousins Tiffany I love you for everything you do for me, seen and unseen. Thank you always!!

A special thank you to Nikki Brown... you continue to help me whenever I ask. I am forever thankful to you.

Author Tina J man you drop knowledge on me daily and I hope to be where you are on them charts one day. Thank you for your kindness. Love ya babe!!!

My boo Asia Sparrow I love you boo and we bout to take over this industry.

LaToya Nicole man listen I love you boo, you are one of a kind. You never hesitate to help me out and I thank you for that. Keep rocking them charts boo, but I'm coming lol

Author Belleza, thank you for all your help no matter what it is I ask for.

Tamia Mills I know we get on your nerves, but I truly thank you for everything you do for the team. You do it without breaking a sweat. I can't wait to see what life has in store for you because you are destined for greatness.

To the synopsis queen Erica, hats off to you girl 'cause you are the ish!! Thank you!!

K.C Mills thank you for taking a chance on lil' ole me. I hope I make you proud Boss Lady, I'm tryna be like you when I grow up. LOL

Thank you to my loves Shameeka James, Bria Chanel, Kiera

LaShy, and SeQuoya for test reading and helping me whenever I need you guys.

To the readers thank you for giving me a chance. It gets better!!

Thank you to any and every body that has supported me, shared my post, and mentioned my book to somebody, etc. thank you thank you thank you.

To all my Lupus warriors out here… keep fighting we got this!!! FUCK LUPUS!!!!!

Y'all know my mind be all over the place, so if I forgot anybody, just add your name here _____!!!!!!!!

SHE READDDDYYYY!!!!!!!!

SYNOPSIS

Part one of My Heart Beats for an Atlanta Boss was full of drama for Nautica, Amaris and Ahnais. Things finally started going well for the trio and then it quickly spiraled out of control.

Nautica's past comes back with a vengeance and Majik vows to do whatever to keep her safe. When the unthinkable happens will Majik and Nautica's relationship survive or will Nautica end up back in the same situation she tried so hard to escape?

Ahnais' rapist is closer to home that she realized and it has become a distraction to her engagement to Draiven. She wants nothing more than to plan the wedding of her dreams but how can she when her rapist is still out lurking? Draiven knows that he can keep Ahnais safe and that she has nothing to fear but the doubt in her eyes is still present. Can Draiven really keep Ahnais safe? Will a tragic past keep her from moving on to an amazing future?

Amaris and Jaysun faced a horrible tragedy in the first installment that they have not fully recovered from. The couple is given some more shocking news that makes their already stressful relationship even rockier and the couple may not recover from it. Can Amaris and Jaysun come together to defeat the conflicts in their relationship or has too much happened for them to move forward?

All three couples have work to do in order to make it past hard times. The road will be rough and one of these couples just might not be a couple in the end. When it's all over will these three Hearts still beat for an Atlanta Boss?

WHERE WE LEFT OFF...

I felt like I was about to lose my mind. I'd been running around for days tryna get shit together for this dinner I had planned for Ahnais. She been having an attitude since yesterday, of course she thinking I'm up to no good. I had one thing left I needed to handle before the dinner tomorrow and that was this Tatiana situation.

I was on the way to meet Majik and Lenyx, so I could finally get this shit over with. This bitch has been a pain in my ass ever since she drugged me. Calling my phone threatening me, tryna expose me not knowing my girl already know. I just been going along with the shit. I pulled up to Lenyx house with my all black on ready for war. Knowing I was about to end this bitch was enough to make my dick hard. I walked in his shit like I owned it; I was just waiting for him to say something smart.

"Nigga don't be walking yo Ron Stoppable looking ass in my

shit like you pay bills," he said walking in the living room with the phone glued to his ear.

Ever since we had the lil barbecue at my house a few weeks ago, his ass ain't been doing shit but up Selina ass. I hope he checked her out because I won't mind putting a bullet in her head if she on some fuck shit.

"I'll burn this shit down with yo *Casper the friendly ghost* looking ass in it," he swung tryna hit me and I ducked. "Aight keep on with yo light bright ass and I'mma clap you the fuck off."

I had Majik dying laughing and Len couldn't say shit, he just shot me a bird and went back to caking. I got in a game of NBA 2K18 with Majik until it was time to go handle business.

It was finally one a.m. and we loaded up in the chop shop car we got so it couldn't be traced. Shit was gonna be ashes after this was over with anyway. We came up on Tatiana's house and scoped the scene. Them muthafuckas had her living it up. I cut the electricity off and Lenyx was able to pick through the lock. It was dark as hell but with the night googles we copped, we were able to see everything.

Going from room to room we finally came up on the one she was in. This bitch was knocked out all peacefully like her life wasn't in danger. I had Len cut the lights back on cause I needed this bitch to see my face before I killed her ass.

"Wakey wakey lil' bitty bitch," tapping her forehead with my pistol to wake her up out her sleep.

She jumped up looking around. When her eyes focused and landed on me fear took over and she tried to scream.

"Scream and I'mma make sure to kill you nice and slow."

"Wait Draiven, you don't have to do this! I'm sorry; I promise I'll leave you alone!"

"What happened to that tough girl shit?"

She sat there crying like that shit was supposed to move me. I didn't give a damn bout them tears.

"Tell me what you know about them muthafuckas you work for." Majik said.

"I-I um, I don't know what you're talking about."

Before she got the words out, Majik shot her in the arm. "Ahhhhh! Ok, ok!"

"Stop fucking playing with me bitch. I can do this shit all night."

"There isn't much I can tell you. I've been working for them for years and was told to get close to y'all. I was told to disrupt your home and throw you off your square. I don't know what they have planned for y'all but they coming hard."

This bitch wasn't telling me shit and I was tired of playing with her.

"How many times did you text me trying to blackmail me?" She shrugged her shoulders looking stupid. "Look at your phone and see."

She grabbed her phone and I stood next to her to make sure she wasn't tryin' no funny shit.

"Twelve, it was twelve times."

"Alright then," I said as I shot her in the other arm.

I ignored her screams as I continued to shoot her in different parts of her body. I made sure to shoot her in places that would kill her slowly. She was still alive, barely hanging on. For the final twelfth shot, I hit her with a head shot that damn near took her head off. Turning on her stove and the gas, we got the fuck up out of there and before we turned the corner her shit exploded. It was no way that body would be found. Once we made it back to Lenyx's house I jumped in my car and took my ass home. I was relieved that shit was finally over.

I woke up the next day nervous as hell. Tonight, was the night and I needed everything to go off as planned. I called the restaurant twice to make sure everything was set up the way I asked. Ahnais had to go into work for a few hours today so I sent her a text letting her know we had dinner with the family tonight. Of course, she thought it celebrating one of our problems being handled. After I got the confirmation that everything was in order, I chilled around the house for the remainder of the day.

Later that night…

I jumped in the shower and handled my hygiene; I'd been lying around all day, so I know my nuts was funky. I planned on being knee deep in my girl's guts tonight, so I needed to be good and fresh. It didn't take me long to wash my ass, lotion up, and throw on my clothes I had hanging up in the closet. I had bought all of us some shit to wear tonight, we were about to be on our fly shit.

Of course, Ahnais was taking all got damn day to get ready. We were gonna be late for our own damn dinner reservation if she didn't hurry up.

"Ahnais, what the hell is taking you so long? You've had plenty of time to get ready man!"

"Chill out damn, I'm almost ready. I just gotta change purses."

Twenty minutes later we were finally walking out the door. It didn't take long for us to make it to the restaurant, so we were pulling up in no time. I was breaking all kind of laws getting us there. I'm glad Mama Frankie had ridden with Amaris or she'd be cussing my ass the fuck out.

I let the hostess know we had a reservation and she led us to the private room they'd set up. Everyone was already here, and I was glad. I wanted to get this shit over with as quick as possible. My damn stomach was doing all kind of flips and I was farting like a muthafucka.

"Auntie you look so pretty!" Majesti came up to her and said.

"Thank you, baby, so do you!" She kissed her on the cheek and she ran back to her seat.

"Sis, I know you glad that bitch is out the way," Amaris said taking a sip of her drink.

"Girl I was bout ready to get at that bitch myself."

"I know how you feel cause I'm bout ready to take me out a bitch," Nautica spoke up giving Majik a mean ass mug.

"Don't start that shit man."

Ain't no telling what that shit was about. CoCo known for doing stupid ass shit, so it wasn't no telling.

We had gotten through our meal and it was that time. I was sweating like a hoe in church. I gave the waitress the signal to let her know it was that time.

The music started playing and I had my homeboy Shawn come out singing. That was a true gangsta through and through, but he could sing his ass off.

I found love in you
And I've learned to love me too
Never have I felt that I could be all that you see
It's like our hearts have intertwined and to the perfect harmony

I stood up just when the song was coming to an end as Ahnais looked around trying to figure out what was going on. Getting on my knee I began to speak from my heart. "Oh my God! Oh my God! Oh my God!" she said bouncing up and down.

"I told you when we first met that I would one day make you my wife. You have made me a better man and I can't imagine living life without you. Every day I imagine what it will be like to grow old with you and raise a shitload of kids that look just like you. You are the most beautiful woman I've ever seen. I want to spend the rest of my life loving you, providing for you, and being the man you want me to be. Ahnais Janae Davenport will you marry me?"

Pulling the ring box from my pocket, I opened it as I looked up at her and wiped the tears that were falling from her eyes.

"Yes, yes, yes!"

Standing up I hugged her lifting her off her feet. I wasn't done yet though. I had one more thing I needed to do. Walking over to my baby girl Yanni, I got back on my knee, and grabbed her hand.

"What are you doing daddy?"

"The first day you called me daddy was one of the best days of my life. I'd never imagined having a daughter as beautiful as you. I want to spend the rest of my life loving you, teaching you, guiding you, and showing you how a man is supposed to treat you. If you will have me, I want to officially be your daddy and give you my last name. What you say kiddo, can I be your daddy?"

"That means I'll have you and mommy's name?"

"That's right baby girl."

She leaped in my arms and wrapped her arms around my neck as tight as she could. I kissed the side of her head and hugged her back.

"I love you daddy."

"Love you more Yanni."

I handed her mother the adoption papers that I had gotten. I'd already filled out my part, I just needed her to fill out hers.

Everyone stood up congratulating us and the girls of course were giving me their don't fuck up speeches. We were standing around chopping it up in our on world when we were interrupted by the sounds of someone clapping.

Clap clap clap clap

"That was a beautiful proposal my nigga, I hope y'all can come to me and my girls wedding soon. Ain't that right Nautica?"

I don't know who the fuck this nigga was, but he was bout to get his ass killed.

"Yo who the fuck is this bitch ass muthafucka?" Majik asked Nautica pulling out his Glock.

"Draego," she whispered and moved behind him scared.

Shit he pulled out his strap and me and Lenyx did the same. I felt Ahnais shaking and I turn to look at her and she was crying with nothing but fear in her eyes.

"Babe why are you shaking, what's the matter?"

"That's him, that's him, that's the man that raped me!" she said and fainted.

What the fuck?

NAUTICA

I couldn't believe I was looking at the devil himself. Never in a million years did I expect him to come in like this. The look on Majik's face was one of pure hate. I could see his jaw twitching and trigger finger itching.

"Hey baby you ain't gonna speak to ya man?" Draego with a sneaky smile asked.

"Why are you here? I have nothing for you."

"You know why I'm here. I came to get what's mine."

"Nigga you ain't come to get shit except your name in the obituary section," Majik spoke up.

I looked around at the many guns that were pointed at Draego and I knew this shit was about to end all bad. The last thing I wanted or needed was for any one of them to end up in jail. We were in a closed off area, so I don't even know how the hell he got in here without being noticed.

"Oh, that's where you're wrong. Legally she's mine." He crossed his arms over his chest with a sinister smirk on his face.

"What the hell are you talking about?" I had an uneasy feeling in my stomach just that quick.

"You'll find out in due time."

"Excuse me is there a problem? I need to advise you that the police have been called."

This is exactly what the fuck I was afraid of. At this point I didn't give a damn about the police because my damn cousin was still passed out and I needed to check on her. The last thing she said was that he raped her.

Draiven had been trying to wake her up for the last five minutes. Amaris had been telling them to call an ambulance but them fools still hadn't done it.

"No there ain't no problem here. Let me holla at your manager," Majik demanded.

"I'll let y'all get back to your little gathering, I'll be in touch Nautica." He turned to walk out I assumed the way he came in.

The guys put their guns up and Majik went to have a word with the manager. I'd like to know how the hell Draego was able to even come in here and nobody stopped him. Once I saw the manager being handed money I knew shit was all good and the cops wouldn't step foot in this room.

Draiven finally was able to wake Ahnais up but when she sat up she was looking all around the room.

"Ahnais, what the hell? Are you okay?" I tried to give her a sip of water, but she pushed my hand away.

"Did you know?" Sobbing loudly, she asked me. I was confused as to what the hell she was talking about.

"Umm, did I know what?"

"That's the man, that's the man that raped me! Did you know?" She was getting a little too loud for my liking and I wasn't feeling that shit.

"Why would you think I'd knowingly fuck with a man that raped my cousin? That's some straight up bullshit!"

I was getting pissed cause I didn't like what the hell she was insinuating. If I knew he'd raped her I would have told that shit or killed his ass myself. She really got me fucked up.

"Come on y'all tripping. Ahnais, don't do that, you know Nautica wouldn't be on no foul shit like that," Amaris spoke up trying to diffuse the argument we all knew was about to happen.

"Look y'all chill out, we gonna take this shit back to Mama Frankie's crib, y'all know better than speaking in public and in front of these kids." Lenyx pointed out what I had forgotten all about.

Looking over at Majesti, she was all in the conversation and of course Yanni's grown ass wasn't missing a beat.

After Draiven cleared up the tab, everyone got in their cars and headed over to my Auntie's house. I could tell Majik was pissed because his jaw was twitching up a storm and he hadn't said much.

I made sure Majesti had on her headphones and put on one of her movies before I said anything.

"Are you mad at me about something?"

He looked at me out the corner of his eye and still didn't say anything. I really would like to know what the fuck his problem is. It ain't like he didn't know the motherfucka was lurking. I was about to go in on his ass but of course he had to pull up to my Auntie's house at the same time. Normally I'd wait for him to open my door, but I jumped out, got Maji out her seat and went in ahead of him. The way I slammed the door, he now knew I was pissed.

Since everyone pretty much got here at the same time, I took Maji in the spare room with Yanni. It was the weekend, but I always tried to keep her on somewhat of a schedule when I'm around. It was getting pretty late and she needed to lie down.

I took my ass out on the porch and ordered me an Uber. I be damn if I was gonna sit here while Ahnais accuse me of some bullshit and Majik side eyeing me. Nope they both got me fucked up.

"Why you sitting out here? We waiting on yo ass."

"I just ordered me an Uber, I be damn if I sit up in there and be accused of shit and then Majik's big built body ass looking at me all sideways and shit. Nah I been done cussed both they asses out."

Just thinking about it had me hot. Shit, I get how Ahnais is feeling, but did she forget I was the one getting my ass beat by Draego for years? I was so damn mad, I almost got up and served both of them these hands.

"Girl don't let that shit get to you. We just need to figure this bullshit out."

Before I could give her a response, a car was pulling up. The shit had me on edge, I was breaking my neck to see who it was.

Just as I was about to run my paranoid ass in the house, I got a text that my Uber was here. I hugged Amaris and made my way to the car.

"Aye my man, she straight." Majik slightly pushed me to the side and closed the door back. "Why you keep tryna piss me off man? Why would your stupid ass go getting into cars with strange muthafuckas knowing yo' bitch ass ex on the loose?"

"Oh, now you can fucking talk!" I wasn't thinking about his ass at this point. I went around him and tried to get in anyway.

"Keep on with the dumb shit Nautica!"

"Are you okay ma'am?" The Uber driver asked concerned.

"Man get yo ass up outta here tryna play captain save em, for yo ass need saving."

I couldn't stand a scary ass man. Mutombo's ass got the hell up out of there with the quickness. I could have been in some real danger.

"You just keep on doing childish and dumb shit. Why would u get in a fucking car with someone you don't know, knowing all this shit going on? That muthafucka could be lurking around the corner right got damn now. You need to start taking this shit serious."

"What the fuck did I do to you? Okay, I get I didn't think about jumping in a car with a stranger, but you been on some funny acting shit ever since we left the restaurant."

I couldn't wait to hear what he had to say. Before he could say anything Majesti came out on the porch looking tired and sleepy.

"Nauti, when are we going home? Grandma Frankie's bed isn't soft enough."

Shit, I'd forgotten that I promised her I was staying with them tonight. She already deals with one deadbeat of a mother, I didn't want to break any promises to her. At the same time, I didn't want to be around her punk ass daddy at the moment.

"In a minute Majesti, go back in the room for a little while."

"You need to chill the fuck out. Look, I was pissed cause I couldn't handle that fuck nigga. I'd been looking for his ass and he was able to one up me. That shit ain't supposed to happen to a nigga like me. I'm supposed to protect my family."

"So, you take it out on me instead of talking about it?"

"I'm saying my bad."

See he got shit all the way out of order if he thinks I'm about to accept that half ass apology. I walked off towards the house and left him standing right where he was. Until he delivers a better apology, he can talk to my back.

I went in the living room where everyone was and took a seat. I had so much shit running through my mind, it was hard for me to focus on what was going on. I was wracking my brain trying to figure out what Draego meant by I was technically his.

AHNAIS

I never expected to see that man again, but I knew I'd recognize him if I ever did. Seeing him brought on so much pain that I had buried a long time ago. His voice, his eyes, and even his scent was embedded back in my mind. I didn't mean to take it out on Nautica, but it blew my mind finding out that the same man she'd been running from is the same man that raped me. I'd never give him the title of Yanni's father, because that bastard would never get to know my child. This world is too fucking small, I gotta have bad luck or no luck at all. How in the hell did she end up with him is what I want to know?

I walked up to her and I could tell she was still in her feelings. She had her arms crossed, lips poked out and eyes rolling up in her head.

"Can I talk to you for a minute cuz?"

"Talk!" She frowned her face up leaned her head to the side. If she wasn't family that shit would've had us over here fighting.

"I'm sorry, I had no right to accuse you of anything. I know you wouldn't ever do any foul shit like that." I was getting emotional thinking about everything.

I knew she wanted to come out her mouth with some slick shit but once I broke down the look on her face softened up.

"Don't try me like that again Ahnais."

I reached for a hug without responding to what she'd said. I was in the wrong and I can't be mad at how she feels and reacts.

It was really bugging me that she was with a rapist and I had to ask her how she'd even met him.

"Nautica, I just have a question? How did you meet him?"

"I was out with a few ladies from work one night after our shift. He approached our table and asked for my number. In getting to know him, he did tell me that he was from Atlanta. I found it a little strange that every time I asked him to come with me to Atlanta, he'd always find an excuse as to why he couldn't. I wondered all the time why wouldn't he want to visit his family, but I didn't think too much of it."

I heard everything she said, but the only thing that registered in my mind was that he was close. What if he found out about Yanni and tried to take my baby?

"Draiven, what about my baby? What if he finds out Yanni is his and try to take her?" I started hyperventilating just from the thought alone.

"First of all, shawty, calm the fuck down. I wish you would let another man get you bothered. Second of all, don't ever let him being her father come out your mouth. That's my got damn child and don't you forget that shit!"

I stopped in the middle of trying to catch my breath and switched gears real quick.

"Nigga you better remember who you damn talking to. All that shit ain't necessary. You know what the hell I'm getting at."

Shit, I wasn't that gone that I couldn't come back and check his ass.

I didn't mean anything by saying Draego was my child's father. He knew what the fuck I was trying to say.

With all this shit going on, I couldn't even enjoy and celebrate my engagement. This is what I've been waiting for and I couldn't be happy.

"All y'all bosses in this room, how y'all weak asses let that nigga one up y'all?" my mama lit a cigarette and asked.

This was not the time for my mama to be on her usual bullshit. On some real shit, I wanted to know the same thing.

"The end result is all that matters," Majik smoothly answered. "Look it's been a long ass night, we gonna get back up tomorrow and settle this shit. We got some other bullshit to run by y'all anyway."

The Next Day....
I was still in my feelings and I didn't wanna do shit today but spend time with my daughter. I felt like I needed to apologize again to Nautica for my actions last night.

I found my phone on my nightstand and called her up.

"What you want Ahnais? You know I don't wake up early on my off days." It was almost eleven in the morning and she talking like I called her at the crack of dawn.

"I'm taking Yanni with me today for some girl time at the nail shop and we hitting up the mall. You wanna get Majesti and meet us?"

"She was supposed to go home today, let me have Majik make sure CoCo ain't have nothing planned for her." This crazy ass girl started laughing when she said that.

She and I both know CoCo ain't tryna do shit with her damn child. I chatted it up with Nautica for a little while longer and then got up to get my day started. Two minutes later I got a text from her saying that they'd kick it with us today. I'd already known that was gonna be the answer, so I wasn't the least bit surprised.

I needed to get a move on cause they would be here in two hours and I would need all that time. I wouldn't dare get caught out in these streets looking a mess. We were riding together, and I'd pissed Nauti off already for the week. Her ass hated to have to wait on somebody. After I went to check on Yanni's outfit of choice for the day, it was time to search for something to wear for myself. I was gonna keep it simple and throw on a sleeveless white body suit with *IDGAF* written across it, ripped black jeans and my black and white Vans. It made for a perfect mall outfit.

After I was done with my shower, I beat my face to the gawds and before I knew it, my doorbell was ringing. Luckily, I'd just gotten done so I didn't have to worry about hearing Nautica complain.

"Hey Tee Tee, you ready to tear the mall down? It's a must I go in Justice. Justine in my class came to school Friday with a new outfit on and she thought she was all that." Majesti rolled her eyes like she could just imagine it all over again. I don't know what they teaching these kids nowadays but they grown ass hell, mine included. But I can't even front, she's just like me.

"Lil cuz forget Justice we rocking Gucci Monday morning. Tuh she thought!" I spit out my water laughing at Yanni. These lil' heffas were something else.

We jumped in the car with Nautica and made our way to the nail shop. It wasn't nothing but a good time as we bobbed our heads to that old school *Tupac*. I always felt like a true gangsta after listening to some *Pac*. It wasn't packed like I thought it'd be on Saturday afternoon, which was odd to me, but hey I wasn't complaining at all. I let Yanni pick the color she wanted, and I picked mine.

It was hit or miss with her, I never knew when she'd be in her tomboy mood. Luckily for me, she was in her girly girl stage. It wasn't too often that I could get my nails done like I wanted them. Being the head Pharmacist, I was constantly working, and long nails could get in the way. I had seven days off and I was bout to take advantage of it.

After spending damn near three hours in the nail shop, I was passed ready to fucking go. I was two seconds from calling the mall trip off. Being that it wasn't even four blocks over and I had shit I needed to get, I continued on with my outing.

I needed to put a little bit in my stomach before I shopped my ass off, so I stopped at the little pretzel stand outside the food court. They got some good little mini cinnamon pretzels. I was in the midst of fucking them shits up when I ran smack dead into someone.

My whole snack went on the ground. I was trying not to get pissed off, but I was hungry as hell.

"My bad beautiful, I should have been watching where I was going."

I was looking at my pile of food on the floor and when I looked up, my breath got caught in my throat. Standing before me was one fine ass man. He had to be mixed with something, but I knew he had some Italian somewhere in his blood.

"Well you weren't and now my food is on the floor!" Even though I'm sure it's partly my fault, I'm not gonna let him off the hook.

"How about you let me take you out for a real meal as an apology?"

Before I could even let him down Yanni decided to speak up for me.

"No thank you, we don't eat out. My daddy umm her husband, don't want us talking to strangers. Have a good time eating alone though."

Nautica and Majesti had a good ole laugh from Yanni's ass as she pulled me in the opposite direction of Mr. Fine. I almost beat her ass cause I wasn't able to get me another order of them shits. Just as I was about to cuss her out Draiven was calling me.

"Yes darling?"

"Don't get niggas killed out here, stop grinning and shit in these niggas' faces."

"Boy what is you talking about? I started looking all around expecting him to pop out from somewhere.

"I'm always watching Ahnais, remember that. I'll holla at you when I get to the crib."

That punk ass nigga hung up on me. I for one want to know how he even knows someone was in my face. That's some shit we about to have a conversation about.

I carried on with my shopping trip and put that in the back of my mind.

I was starting to get weirded out because it seemed every store I went in Mr. Fine was in. I brought it to Nautica's attention and we got the hell up outta there. I didn't need shit happening to us while we had our girls. On the way to the car we both got a text to meet the family back at Mama's house. That only means more bullshit is on the horizon.

Here we fucking go!

MAJIK

If it ain't one thing it's a fucking nother. I'm not surprised this fuck nigga showed up though, I knew the shit was gonna happen. I'm glad his ass is on my turf, it makes it easier for me to be able to kill his ass.

I know Nautica thinks I'm mad at her about all this shit, but honestly, it's just the opposite. I'm mad at my damn self for allowing that lame ass dude to sneak up on us like that. I'm bout to become the fucking connect and shit like this can't happen.

We gotta meet up with Jaysun tonight and speak about merging up with his people. If we become the connect for him and his team on top of what we'll acquire from Marcelo, that shit would bring in a lot of money.

I just need to clean up a few loose ends and handle this lil shit before I take over this muthafuckin world.

I've had Majesti for over a month and her hoe ass mama was

supposed to get her this weekend but that shit ain't happened yet. That cozy little house I bought for her and my baby girl was bout to be snatched from up under her ass. I already cut off her access to Majesti's bank account and she been blowing me up ever since. She wasn't calling about my seed so we ain't have shit to talk about. I'm meeting my lawyer Monday to get full custody, so I won't have to deal with the bitch at all.

I circled around the block of mama Frankie's house a few times to make sure I didn't catch the security slipping. If I caught one of them niggas blinking too long, I'm killing they ass. A muthafucka that's sleep can miss anything.

Frankie was bout to have to tell these girls about that nigga she fucked around with. We can't keep keeping them in the dark. I sat in the car for a few more minutes smoking on this loud pack. I always needed to be faded to deal with this emotional shit I know coming.

After today I was gonna make sure Frankie took her ass back to Draiven's crib until we were able to dead everybody that was after us. She was hardheaded and brought her ass back home, but that was over today. Nautica wouldn't forgive my ass if I let anything happen to her crazy ass auntie.

I walked up in the house high off my ass. I had the munchies and went straight for the kitchen before making my way to the living room where I knew them niggas was hanging out at.

"I know your big swole high yellow ass didn't come in my house eating my shit without speaking first?"

"Don't start today old lady."

"See you light skin people ain't raised right."

We all looked at her like she was crazy. I don't think she realized she was talking about her own damn kids being they ass was just as light.

"You do know your kids' light skin, right?" I had to burst her bubble.

She looked hard for a minute before she answered.

"Just shut the fuck up, why we here any damn way?"

This lady was crazy as hell.

"Our role in these streets are about to change drastically, therefore we need to clear up any loose ends out here. We need y'all to stay alert at all times. Mama Frankie, you need to fill them in, it's time."

I could see she was ready to cuss our asses the fuck out. Shit I didn't care bout that though. If her being mad would keep everybody alive, then so be it.

"This isn't how I wanted to have this conversation with you girls. I need to talk to y'all about the muthafucka that helped bring you in this world. Listen-"

"I thought you didn't know our father!" Amaris stood up and said cutting her off.

I'm glad I smoked that blunt before coming in.

"First off, you can sit your ass the fuck back down and any nigga can nut in you and make a baby, that don't make his ass a father. Now like I was saying about your donor, I met him when I was fourteen years old. To sum it up he's an Italian named Solomon who left me with two kids cause I didn't fit into his world. I was assured by his asshole father Gennaro that if I contacted him or their family that he'd harm you girls. That was after he made sure to introduce me to Solomon's fiancé at the time."

"Why are you telling us this now? We've been asking you who our dad was all our lives?" Ahnais spoke up.

"Listen y'all can have this Oprah moment another time." I wasn't bout to sit here and listen to them hash out their family business. "Y'all pops is after us for some reason and may use y'all to get close. Bottom line keep ya eyes open and don't be talking to muhfuckas you don't know."

I had a few other things to take care of, so I didn't have time to sugarcoat shit. I gave them thirty more minutes of my time before I got up outta there. My main concern was getting at Draego. Once I found out he was out here raping women, it made the hunt for his ass jump up on the top of my list. Not that it wasn't before.

COCO

I been living it up these last few weeks and I won't apologize for it. Not having to deal with Majesti's smart mouth ass was a breath of fresh air. Majik's stupid ass cut off my funds, so he could deal with his child. He had me fucked up though if he thought I was gonna just be okay with him cutting me off.

I didn't have time to think about my get back for my baby daddy right now. I met a sexy ass brown skin dude at the store a few weeks ago and we were finally going out. I'd been talking to him on the phone every chance that I got, and I really liked him. He's been there for me when I need to vent about Majik and Nautica's hoe ass.

I had no idea where he was taking me, but I know I wanted to impress the hell out of him. I missed having a man in my bed every night to wake up to. Good thing about it, he looked like he had money. I don't know if it was my baby daddy money, but he had it.

I wasn't willing to fuck with a man that didn't have any money. I wasn't about to get out here and work, so any man that wanted to get with me better be able to take care of me.

While I was getting my clothes out for my date, my phone started ringing and I was praying it wasn't him canceling on me. I found my phone under a stack of clothes I'd tried on and saw it wasn't nobody but my bestie Kaycie.

"What up bitch?" I answered balancing my phone on my ear with my shoulder. I was still looking in the mirror examining a potential outfit for tonight.

"Girl why you sound outta breath?" she asked popping her gum in my ear. That was so fucking irritating.

"Trying to see what I wanna wear for my date tonight."

"You sure you wanna go out with him?"

Oh, my goodness this bitch was about to irritate me, I feel it in my bones.

"Why wouldn't I? This nigga looks good as hell and look like he balling. Hell yeah I'm bout to snatch him the fuck up."

"I've been around when you talk to him and he seems to ask too many questions about yo baby daddy and his bitch. Don't that seem strange to you?"

"So, what you saying? He's not really interested in me?" I was getting pissed talking to this bitch.

"Why you getting upset CoCo? I'm just being a friend, but hey, whatever."

"Yeah whatever, I'll talk to you later." Hanging up on her, I didn't even wait for her to say bye.

I didn't give that shit she was saying a second thought, I wasn't gonna let her or nobody else ruin this for me. I noticed he asked about Majik a lot, but I'm chalking it up to him just trying to know about the people in my life. Until I find out otherwise, that's what I'm going with.

After handling my business in the bathroom, I made sure I lotioned up my body hella good with the best Bath and Body Works scent I had. Call me what you want, but I was hoping to put this good shit on this nigga tonight. I'm tryna lock his ass down, he's new in town and I didn't need these other bitches getting a chance.

I was in the middle of putting on my shoes when my phone rang again.

"What do you want Majik?" My eyes could've gotten stuck I rolled them up so damn hard.

"Bitch don't act like you doing me a fucking favor by answering yo phone."

"Why you calling me?"

"Man keep playing with me like I won't come smack the fuck outta you. When yo hoe ass planning on seeing your fucking daughter?"

"You acting like the father of the decade over there with yo bitch and shit. I'll see her soon, you got it!"

"I don't know what I ever saw in yo ratchet hoe ass!"

"A pretty face and a pussy to fuck, now you stuck with me for life. I'm forever in them pockets, you might as well open that account back up. It's either give it to me voluntarily or involuntarily when I take your ass to court."

"Bitch you'll die before you touch my money again."

Before I could respond, Majik did what he does best and hung up in my face. It's cool though, he better get all his time with Majesti out cause I'm coming for her and I'll be seeing him in court.

By the time I finished putting the final touches on my makeup and throwing things in my purse, the doorbell was ringing.

Checking myself one more final time I made my way to the door.

"Hey Draego, you're on time, that's a good sign."

I had to put on my good girl act until I locked his ass down.

"What's up ma, you ready to head out?"

"Yeah let me grab my purse."

After I locked up I jumped in his 2018 G-Wagon and I was highly impressed. I made sure I gave him good conversation on the way to Dave and Busters. I wanted to go somewhere that I could eat and have a little fun. I didn't need the fancy shit.

It didn't take but a good thirty minutes to get there and just by the little talk we had, I was already ready to put this pussy on him.

"So, tell me a little about Draego. I know we've been talking by phone, so tell me something you haven't shared with me."

"I'm from Atlanta, got into a little bit of trouble and moved to Chicago for a fresh start."

"What brings you back this way?"

"My ex left me and came to Atlanta. I came here to get her back originally, but now I may not have to do that."

I got a weird feeling when he started speaking about his ex, but I chopped it up to him just being in love and missing her. I wasn't letting his ass get back with whoever the bitch was anyway. This my new meal ticket.

"It's a good thing you won't need your ex now. What's her name anyway?"

"All that ain't important right now. What's good with you though? You never told me why you were single."

"My baby daddy met a new bitch and decided he wanted something different, to sum it up."

"Is that right?" The far off look in his eyes was weird as fuck. "Hmmmm, I guess that's a good thing for the both of us."

We spent about two hours eating, talking, and just getting to know each other. After that we got up and enjoyed a few games.

I was ready to take this little date back to my place. A bitch was real hot in the ass right now.

DRAIVEN

Shit in my house been fucking hectic as hell ever since I found out about Draego's ass. It seemed like he was a thorn in everyone's side. Ahnais has started back having nightmares and I'm pissed cause I can't find him to kill his ass. I know he right up under my nose, but the fuck nigga doing a damn good job of hiding. I feel like I'm trying to find Pokémon.

I'd never thought that Nautica's ex would be the man that raped my girl, but I've always told her that if we ever came across the perverted muthafucka, I wouldn't hesitate to put some hot shit in his ass.

Today I decided to spend some daddy daughter time with Yanni. It's been a minute since I've hung out with my baby girl. With all the bullshit we got coming our way, I never know when it may be my last on this fucking earth. I want my youngin' to always have some type of memories with me if she ever needed it.

We ended up at Atlanta Metro Fun center and it was a lot of shit in here for her to do. Bowling, arcade games, laser tag, you name it they had it.

"Dad what's wrong with mama, you didn't mess up, again did you?"

"It ain't me this time baby girl, but don't worry about that. I got your mama."

"Aight daddy, I guess. I'm going to the bathroom."

I sent out a few important messages while I waited for Yanni to come back. I knew once I was done spending time with her, my night was bout to be filled with a bunch of bullshit. Especially since that nigga Raz was short on our money. Muthafuckas don't know what loyalty is these days.

Yanni had been gone for way too long and I had just got up to get her when I saw her coming back towards the table. She was looking kinda spooked out and I immediately was on alert.

"What you looking crazy for?"

"Somebody stopped me and told me to give you this," she said handing me over a folded-up piece of paper.

You touched something of mine, now be ready for me to touch something of yours.

I jumped up with my Glock in my hand. I didn't give a fuck about these kids in here. Somebody was close to my got damn child. I ran inside the women's bathroom checking to see if anyone was in there.

"Yanni, who gave you this?" I shook her a little too hard, at this point though I needed to find out who the fuck was close to my child.

"I don't know daddy, some white looking man."

"Come on get your shit and let's go. Daddy got something to handle, we'll do this another day."

"Daddy you know all you gotta do is teach me how to shoot. I'm already good with the knife."

"Yanni bring yo' ass on, ion have time to play with you right now. Tell me exactly what the person looked like!"

I grilled her over and over until we made it back to the house. Ahnais and Mama Frankie was told to keep their asses in the house for the rest of the day. I made sure my cameras were working and the niggas I had watching my joint was on point.

Jumping right back in my Dodge Challenger, I peeled out like I was running from the police. I don't know where my ass was going. Lenyx's ass was at the warehouse counting up bricks, so I headed that way.

I'm thinking it was them fuck ass Italians and I was tired of their asses. Somebody was about to die behind approaching my daughter. Three things I don't play with my wife, my kid, and my money.

"Yo something gotta be done 'bout them lasagna muthafuckas!"

"Nigga fuck you doing busting in here like somebody done stole your lunch money?" Majik asked walking from the back with his hand on his strap.

"Fuck you bitch, look at this shit!" I handed them the note that was given to Yanni.

"Yo where the fuck this come from?" Lenyx wanted to know.

"I was out spending time with my shorty and she come back from the bathroom with this bullshit. Muthafucka got close to my child and that's a problem for me!" I was getting pissed the more I thought about it.

"We might can handle the shit sooner than later. I just got a little tip from Marcelo. We can go check it out after we count up these bricks. Aye Len, go back there can get Raz and Tate, this their fucking job."

"Fuck I look like Benson? You do that shit."

Got damn, I didn't have time for these two niggas to go back and forth like they were in a rainbow relationship. I went and got them fools so this work could be done, I needed answers and the quicker we got finished the quicker we could go and check this shit out.

Apparently, some fools that work for Solomon been laying low over Gwinnett County. My first stop was back to the lil fun center to check them cameras. I need to have an accurate picture of who I'm looking for. That's gonna be the first person's head I take off. He fucked up when he came close to my seed.

By the time we had the new shipment separated and ready to go, it was dark as hell outside. That was good for me anyway, folks be on that snitching shit. We didn't need to be out in daylight killing people.

We pulled up to the block we were scoping out and after watching the cameras at the fun center, I had an idea who I was looking for. I was about to make an example out of lil' Mr. bike messenger. I must have smoked about two blunts of that good gas while we watched these niggas move. I was officially on go mode.

Somebody pulled into the driveway in a beat-up old Honda Accord and it was the nigga from the video. Just the muthafucka I wanted. It was go time.

"Aye, that's who I need. It's time to kill these niggas. We been watching long enough!"

"Yo why the fuck is you hollering and spitting in my ear? I got Fizz and them niggas coming through to have our backs. We can't underestimate they asses."

I was on edge, waiting with my finger on the trigger. Once we got word that our backup was here, it was fucking go time.

We used a homeless crackhead decoy to knock on the door and once it opened, I didn't care about shit. They didn't have nothing but about six muthafuckas with them, so I knew we was coming out alive. Two niggas were laid out before we made it to the living room.

Five of us barged in through the front while the rest came in through the back, it's a good thing cause two was caught tryna run, including the fuck nigga I wanted.

"Bring they ass up in here. Tie they ass right there!"

Before I could ask my first question, Majik shot one in the leg.

"That was a warning. I'm tired and not with the bullshit. My girl at home horny with a wet pussy, we want answers and I ain't got time to play."

I swear this nigga got some major issues.

"Did you approach my daughter?"

"Fuck you!"

I shot his ass in the foot. I was feeling like bro, I wasn't up for the bullshit. Just in case he wanted to keep playing, I went ahead and gave him another one in the other foot.

"Ahhhhh fuckkkkk!"

"Quit all the crying like a bitch. You was big boy tough a few seconds ago. Why y'all fucking with us?"

"It ain't my call, we were told to by So-"

"Man shut the fuck up, don't tell they ass shit!" the other brave soul spoke up.

It's always that one in the bunch that wanna play tough. Then it's always that nigga like me that with have to prove them otherwise.

I already knew we wasn't getting nothing outta his ass, so with two shots to the chest and three to the head, that nigga was slumped over before he could get form his next thought.

"Aight, now that that's done, why you approach my kid?"

"Look man, I know you gonna kill me anyway." I took his I.D out his wallet and got his info, he needed a lil push to help him out.

"Do you want your peoples to die with you Josiah Ware at 122 Washington Avenue? I got your name, trust me it won't be hard to find out who your folks are. I'll kill everyone you know including yo dog's playmate from around the corner. Nigga I'll kill your great grandkid's dreams. I ain't in the mood my nigga, start speaking!"

"If I tell you what you wanna know you'll leave my family out of this right?" I cocked my gun back and put it to his head.

He got my point and started talking, "Look Solomon want y'all head on a platter. Y'all about to take over Marcelo's fields in Mexico and he wants him. Y'all too big for him to compete with."

I wonder how the hell he even knew what was about to go down with the transition.

"What beef do that muthafucka got with my wife?"

"Solomon wants to get to know them, but his family want them dead. They are the heir to his empire if anything happens to him, they inherit everything. His kids-"

I jumped back as that nigga's brain splattered everywhere. I noticed a red dot and warned everyone else as I got down.

Gun shots was coming our way quick as fuck. Somebody must've known this man would talk and took his ass out before we could. At least we were able to get a little bit of information. We shot our way out the back door and surprisingly, only lost one worker.

We made it back to our car that was parked in the alley and it wasn't until then that I saw Lenyx was hit in the shoulder. Fuck, it was time to go holla at Doc. It's been a minute since one of us been in this situation. As long as we all alive, my ass ain't bout to complain.

AMARIS

Things had been going about as good as they can go between Jaysun and I. He's been having his bad days a little more frequently lately, but that's to be expected. I'd been sick as hell these last few weeks and what I thought was a bad stomach bug turned out to be a baby. I don't know how the fuck I'm going to tell him this shit. We've only been dating close to a year and with him just losing his daughter, I don't know how he'll take it.

On top of that, I've been stressing about this fucking sperm donor of ours. I have so many questions, like what's his purpose for popping back up, how do you let somebody else keep you from your flesh and blood, and why don't he just choke on a dick and die? That nigga crazy if he thinks we about to have some come to Jesus moment and all will be forgiven. Tuh, I think the fuck not, I still got beef with the bitch Patricia from the second grade that cut in front of me in the lunch line. Oh, let's not forget about Tamika who stepped on my brand-new Reebok classics back in the sixth grade. If I can hold a grudge about some petty shit like that, you already know how this bullshit about to go.

I hadn't talked to my sister in a few days, so I called her to see what she was on.

"Oh, you remembered you got a sister now?" She had a full-blown attitude when she answered the phone.

"Hoe the phone works both ways. What the hell going on with you?"

"Girl if you only knew. Why you sounding like something wrong with you?"

"Stop acting like you know me. Girl-ahhhhhhh how about I done got caught up? A bitch done got pregnant." I sighed just thinking about it, not that it was a bad thing.

"I knowwwww you fucking lying! How you get caught up like that?"

"Chile look, when I tell you this shit snuck up on me like a muthafucka."

"So, what you gonna do? Does Jaysun know?"

"Nah, I haven't had a chance to tell him yet. I really don't know how to though."

"Tell who what?"

I jumped at the sound of Jaysun's voice. I could kick myself right about now. What the fuck was I thinking having this conversation while at this house? I knew better.

"What you talking about babe?" I tried my best to play it off.

"Bitch you caught, call me back tonight if you ain't been killed." Ahnais laughed and hung up.

I personally didn't find shit funny.

"Who you need to tell something to? Stop playing with me Amaris."

"I'm pregnant," I told him in a whisper. I didn't even look up when I said it. I didn't want to see the look on his face, especially if he didn't want this baby.

"When did you find this out?"

"Last week, I thought I was sick with a stomach virus."

"We'll talk about this later, I'll be back." With that he left and that was all I got.

By three in the morning this muthafucka still hadn't come home and I was over the shit. He's never not called if he was gonna come home late if I was staying the night. The more I think about it, I was getting more and more pissed off. I got up and packed my shit I brought over for the night and put my clothes on. I had a helluva lot more shit, but I'd get that later. I jumped in my car and took my ass home.

It took me about thirty minutes to get home and I was sleepy as shit. It was a miracle I made it cause my eyes was heavy as hell.

The next morning...
I don't know what time it was when I rolled over and got up. I fell out as soon as my head hit the pillow.

"Ahhhhh shit!" I screamed at the top of my lungs. I wasn't

expecting for Jaysun weird ass to be sitting in my got damn room. "Nigga, you need to make a sound or something. Why the fuck you sitting in here like a creepy pedophile?"

This man for real sitting in my room in a chair just staring at me and not saying anything. We sat there playing the starring game for about ten minutes before he decided to open his mouth.

"Why you leave our house Amaris?"

I think this nigga done laced his blunt or something cause he talking stupid as hell.

"Umm excuse me playboy, but my house is here. Now if you wanna know why I left your house, it's because you were on the fuck shit when I told you about me being pregnant. I'll never beg a nigga for shit and that includes you."

"You through with your woman's empowerment speech?"

"Whatever Jaysun, what's your purpose for being here? You made it clear how you feel."

"Man shut the fuck up. I ain't made shit clear. Stop fucking just thinking about yourself. I just lost my got damn daughter, don't you think shit hard for me? My child will never meet her brother or sister!"

"I know-" he interrupted me with the quickness.

"Nah you shut yo ass up, you done said what you wanted to say. If I didn't see a forever with you, I damn sho wouldn't have been fucking you without a jimmy. I don't get down like that. If you can't understand that I miss my fucking child and had a moment, I don't know what to tell you. But I know one muthafuckin thing, don't ever leave out by yourself in the middle of the night again. You moving like niggas ain't after yo' ass, stop doing stupid ass shit shawty. Make a fucking appointment tomorrow so we can go check on my seed."

"You ain't gonna be talking to me like you crazy." I rolled my eyes cause that's the only thing I could think of to say and it pissed me off.

I could normally argue a person down, but his ass had me on mute. I was feeling like a five-year-old, ready to pout and shit.

"I'm tired Maris, move yo ass over so I can lay down and shut up shawty."

I'mma move over and shut up for now, but I bet later I'mma be talking again.

I ended up making a doctor's appointment like Jaysun asked, but we had to wait two fucking weeks. I thought about finding another OB GYN, however I'd heard that this was the best damn doctor in Atlanta. So here we are waiting to go back in the room.

This baby daddy of mine had really been on one since I told him about the pregnancy. He's read everything he could on things to prevent cancer in the baby. I've eaten enough oranges and bananas in the last two weeks to last a damn lifetime. Our name was finally called, and I was happy to get this over with.

They took my weight, drew my blood, and placed us in a room. I could see the nervousness on Jaysun's face.

"Hello Amaris, I'm doctor Patel. How are you doing today?"

"I'm doing great, thanks for asking."

"This must be dad?"

"Yes, this is Jaysun, my overbearing child's father."

The doctor laughed, but he had no idea how serious I was. Doctor Patel found out what I meant about Jaysun's overbearing ways after being in there with him for over an hour answering question after question.

"So, Doc, what you saying is in about four months, you can do an amniocentesis?"

I couldn't do shit but put my head down, I was so fucking embarrassed. The doctor was laughing so hard, he couldn't even answer the question.

"Amniocentesis, but yes sir we can do that around the fourth month mark," Doctor Patel corrected him and answered his question.

"Can you test for cancer and things like that with that test?"

"You can't test for cancer in the fetus until it's born. Is there a concern for cancer?"

"My eight-year-old just passed away from Leukemia, I don't want a repeat."

"I'm sorry for your loss. The baby will receive a series of test once he or she is born."

"Yo doc I'm good on the condolences, I just wanna make sure my baby will be straight."

Once the doctor assured us that as of now we had a healthy baby forming inside of me, I got my prenatal prescription, some nausea medicine just in case, and we were out the door.

I could still see concern in his eyes, but I couldn't predict the future so there was nothing I could do at this point. We will just have to see what happens.

LENYX

My ass didn't think I'd be ready for another relationship after Tori's snitching ass. I can't trust these hoes out here. I gotta say Selina been on the up and up. I made sure to check her fucking background a few times before I let my guard down one third of the way.

We done been out on a few dates and talking heavy for a few months now. The crew seem to like her ass, so that was always a good sign. Ahnais was the main one trying to push us to get together. Selina wasn't out here pocket chasing, so it made it that much easier to give her a chance in the beginning. Unlike Tori, she had her own shit and didn't need a man to help her.

Since I was done running around earlier than I had planned, I hit up Selina to see if she wanted to grab some food later and she said it was a go.

I'd just gotten out of the shower and was in my closet

looking for a fresh ass outfit to throw on, when I heard loud ass banging on my door. The only thing I had wrapped around my waist was a towel, but I didn't give a damn. Somebody was beating on my fucking door like they had a problem and I was about to give it to them.

I grabbed my 9 mm from the side table close to my front door and opened it. Fuck putting on some clothes.

I was even more irritated when I peeped Tori's mama and some off-brand ass nigga on the other side of my shit.

"What the fuck is you doing banging on my shit like that for? Fuck you want man?"

"I wanna know where the hell is my daughter? You can lie to the police, but I know you know where she is. I just want my baby. At least tell us where her body is, she deserves a proper funeral." This lady was doing that ugly ass cry and that was irritating my ass like no other.

"Listen lady, I done told you I don't know where that bitch at and I don't give no fucks. You got one more time to approach me bout this bullshit."

"Aye muthafucka, don't disrespect my muthafuckin auntie nigga!" This mark ass clown tryna poke his chest out and act tough.

I got something for niggas that wanna act hard. I put my gun to his head to and waited for him to continue on with the tough guy act.

"Now what was that shit you was saying? Nigga I'll kill your ass with this towel wrapped around my waist, no boxers on, with my dick swinging."

That's what's wrong with muthafuckas out here in these streets, everybody wanna play bad until it's go time. Niggas really don't want no smoke. This bitch made nigga was on mute and ain't said shit since I put the chopper to his dome.

"Dude, all this ain't necessary, we just want to know where my cousin at."

"I ain't ya got damn dude. I told ya'll several times I don't know where her ass at. This gonna be the last muthafuckin time I say the shit. I'm real throwed off in the head, stop playing with me."

"If you hear anything from her, can you please let us know or have her contact us?" Her mama was still shedding them weak ass tears, but she got some act right about herself.

I didn't even give them the courtesy of responding, I closed the door in their face and took my ass back upstairs to finish getting dressed.

I felt like being on my pretty boy shit tonight, so I threw on my fly ass black and white Versace shirt, black washed Versace jeans and my high-top Louboutin sneakers. I even went as far as spraying on a little Tom Ford cologne. I grabbed my keys, the rest of my shit, and walked my handsome ass out the door like I was the shit. Fuck them light skinned niggas on the Golden State Warriors team, I was about to be the new face of light skin men.

I had no idea where I wanted to take this chic, so I was just gonna wing it. It was a good thing I had three sisters though. I shot Amaris a quick text and by the time I pulled up to Selina's house, Amaris had everything in line for me.

I rang the doorbell and waited for her to come to the door.

When she finally opened it up, her ass took my breath away. It's not like I didn't know she was fine, but shawty had my mind gone.

"Damn ma, what you tryna do to a nigga?"

"I guess that means I don't look half bad?"

"Ehh, I guess you'll do, you aight." I pulled her into me and stuck my tongue down her throat.

It was something about the way she was looking tonight that had my dick on go. I was definitely gonna have to get me a random to smash tonight. I already know her ass ain't letting a nigga smash, she been on that let's get to know each other better bullshit.

I was on my gentleman shit, so I opened the door and held it for her as she got in the car. The conversation was flowing while we headed to the spot for dinner.

It took us about forty-five minutes to get to the restaurant. Amaris hooked me up with reservations at Morton's steakhouse over on Peachtree Center Avenue. There wasn't a wait at all and we were seated right away.

"I bet you glad you dropped your attitude and gave a fine nigga like me a chance. You almost missed out."

"What I almost miss out on, huh?"

She licked her lips and that shit sent me over the edge.

"Aye shawty, you gonna have to stop it with all the fuck me faces. I'mma been done bent you over and gave you this dick."

"Hmmmm is that right?" This broad bit her bottom lip while rubbing my dick with her foot.

I'm tryna figure out when she even took her shoes off, but I warned her ass. She better not say shit when I have her walking fucking bowlegged tonight. I been on go for over a week tryna make sure money flowing in right and making sure the family stay alive, I'm backed up like a muthafucka.

"See, when a nigga tries be on his gentlemen shit, you over there on some bullshit."

"Maybe I don't want you to be a gentleman tonight."

I wish she would have said something before I went through all the trouble of getting reservations to this damn restaurant. Since we had already ordered our food, I called the funny looking blonde-haired waitress over and had her box our food up to go and asked for the check.

She looked at me like I was crazy and was bout two seconds from getting her ass cussed out. This bitch acted like it wasn't common for people to have emergencies. I paid my bill, grabbed our food, and pulled Selina's to the car like my ass was on fire.

"What are you doing?" Selina asked laughing.

Wasn't shit funny, she was about to get what she asked for.

My house was at least forty-five minutes away, so I pulled into the nearest five-star hotel I saw.

"Let's go!" I handed my keys to the valet guy and ushered her on in.

She was walking all slow, I guess her ass had time to think about what she done got herself into. It was too late for all that though.

I checked in and we made it to the room and I had nothing but swelling up her uterus on my brain. She sat on the bed to take off her shoes, but I stopped her. Them heels was sexy as fuck and gonna look good on her feet while I had her legs in the air.

"Nah ma, you can leave them shits on."

Before she had a chance to say something back, I pulled shawty up from the bed and started nibbling and kissing her neck and earlobe, while using the other hand to unzip her dress. Once it dropped on the floor, I quickly unsnapped her bra and stuck my hand in her panties. I rubbed in her clit and stuck two fingers inside her pussy.

That shit was good and wet already, so I know shawty had some fire.

"Ooohh Lenyx! Mmmmm wait!" She was biting the shit out of her lip and I haven't even gotten started for real yet.

I sped my hand a little and continued playing with her clit.

Just as she was on the verge of cumming, I stopped and lifted her up on the bar area of the room. Sitting her on the edge, I made sure she had her legs open as far as they could go.

I held her pussy lips open and dove in, face first. A nigga was sucking them juices outta her like she was fresh fruit.

"No! Noooooooo! Ahhhhh! Fuckkkk! I can't take it!"

Her ass was confusing the hell outta me. She saying no but throwing that pussy in my mouth.

"You saying no, you want me to stop?" I asked and at the same time licked on that clit so good, I know she was praying to the heavens above.

She gave me the *'Nigga I wish the fuck you would look'*. I continued on and made her cum for me about two times before I got up to give her this dick.

"You sure you ready for this?" I dropped my drawers and started putting a jimmy on. She was fine and all, but I wasn't running up in nobody raw. I needed her to see what she was about to get. I didn't need her changing her mind at the last minute.

Her eyes bucked big as hell. That ain't the first time I've gotten that reaction. I guess these women out here ain't use to fucking niggas with big dicks.

"Ye umm yeah, I'm ready."

I lifted her off the bar area and carried her to the bed. I tongued her down and tried to calm the uneasiness I saw in her eyes. I mean I was about to murder this pussy, but shawty needed to chill the fuck out. I was gonna bless somebody else with the dick tonight, she the one that kept fucking with me.

Grabbing her ankles, I pulled her slightly to the edge of the bed, pushed both her legs back folding her ass up like a pretzel, and went to work.

If I was a sucka ass nigga, I probably would have dropped a tear and asked her to marry my ass. I had to hold my breath as soon as I stuck my dick in, that's how good her pussy felt.

I wasn't bout to go out like a simp though, I regrouped and went to work.

"Oooh shit, fuuuuucckkkkk. Mmmmm baby, Zaddy, mmm Len, Lenn. Dammit what the fuck is your name?"

"Let me beat this pussy up a lil harder until you can remember."

I flipped her over and put her on her knees, making her give me that perfect arch. I had to shake my head this shit was feeling that good. I was glad she couldn't see me.

She was in trouble once I grabbed a little bit of her hair and wrapped it in my hand. I used the other one to hold her by the waist and began giving her them long deep strokes.

My ass was tryna be hard and not say shit, but it was all over when she started throwing that soft ass back at me. That bullshit almost took me out.

"Fuckkkk, got dammit girl. Fuck you doing?"

We'd been going at it for the last forty minutes and I was ready to let this first nut go.

"Shit Lenyx, mmmmm fuck me daddy!"

She messed up and squeezed my dick with her pussy muscles and it was a wrap. A nigga nutted so hard I think I broke my fucking toes from squeezing them shits so hard.

I know she think it's over, but I'm just getting started. I was nice enough to let her catch her breath for about five minutes and after that I was right back in it.

We must have fucked for about two hours straight and I know I got about six nuts up out her ass. Her screaming my name was the last thing I remembered before I fell a fucking sleep.

One thing I do know is, she gonna have to give up that pussy again. It's too good to try and hold out on.

NAUTICA

Majik was driving me crazy trying to keep up with my every move. I know he's doing it to protect me, but it was driving me crazy. Now that he knows Draego is somewhere around here, he wouldn't even listen to me about the apartment I found.

I didn't help that Amaris' ass was pregnant and staying with Jaysun, cause of course I was forced to stay at his house. It wasn't all bad, but I wanted to be able to say I did something for myself. I messed up telling him I didn't want to stay in a house he once shared with his baby mama, so now he was making me find us a new spot.

I was the type of bitch that didn't need all the extra shit. Give me a bed, food, stuff to wash my ass and I'm satisfied. Majik wanted to buy us this big extravagant ass house. We hadn't been together that long for all that, but I couldn't get that through his head. He claims he knows we'll be together for the long haul. Let him tell it, I didn't have a choice. The fool said if I tried to leave him, he'd kill every nigga that approached me. He said even if he was married with kids, I've been tryna figure that shit out since he said it. How he gonna be happy with another bitch, but kill the niggas that approach me? I guess we both gonna killing muthafuckas, hell if I'm not happy his ass won't be either. He got me fucked up.

We had a little break cause CoCo hoe ass finally decided she wanted to be a mother. Of course, Majesti didn't wanna go, but her dad told her she needed to spend a little time with her mama. I convinced Majik to get her a little phone, so she can always call when she's not with us. I don't trust CoCo and she was too pressed to all of a sudden get her.

I had two more days of work and I would be off for next four days. I done worked for eight days straight and been here since seven this morning. It was time for my break and I hightailed it to the cafeteria. Auntie Frankie cooked a bomb ass meal last night and my fat ass was knocking on their door for a lunch plate.

I warmed up my food in the small break room before I took a seat. Looking on Facebook, I wasn't paying attention to shit that was going on around me. Social media had a way of drawing you in. Someone took it upon themselves to sit with me and it caused me to look up. When I did, I look into the eyes of Draego.

Frantically I glanced around the room, making sure I wasn't in there by myself. This son of a bitch was stupid, but he ain't that damn stupid. I know he ain't tryna go to jail.

"Hey there baby. Did you miss a nigga?"

"Actually, I didn't, I was hoping you died!"

I was pretending like hell that I wasn't scared. I didn't wanna show him no type of fear.

"Look bitch don't act like I won't beat ya ass in here. You know I don't give a fuck about these muthafuckas!"

Casually I grabbed my phone and put it under the table. I knew the buttons I needed to push, and I pressed the number one on speed dial and turned the volume down.

"Draego what is it, what do you want from me? If you really wanted me, you would've done what you needed to do to keep me. I mean you beat my ass every chance you got."

"I don't need a muthafuckin play by play, I know what the fuck I did. You don't end shit, I tell you when it's over and according to this, we ain't never gonna be over."

He handed me an envelope and the curious side of me couldn't help but to open it. Scanning over the documents, I almost passed out at what I was seeing.

"Wha-wa-what is this? How is this possible? There is no way this is legit!" The tears started rolling down my cheeks and I couldn't control it even if I tried.

"I got my ways, so I like I said at your little dinner, you'll always be mine. I think it's time for us to have a bigger wedding. Unless your punk ass nigga wanna pay for your freedom, you stuck with me for the rest of your life. It's till death do us part. I'll be in touch." He got up with the quickness, kissed my cheek, and was gone just as quick as he came.

I wanted to pick up the phone to see if Majik was on there,

but I couldn't pull my eyes away from those documents. I don't know how in the fuck he did it, but according to this shit, I was married to Draego.

I heard Majik on the other end calling my name, but I couldn't talk to him right now. I was too upset and afraid of what he would say. I wasn't expecting Draego to drop that on me. I hit the end button with the quickness just as my big burly ass security detail came running up to me.

"Excuse me Ms. Nautica, boss man said there's a problem in here." He was all out of breath, but he got it out.

"The problem has already left. You missed him."

I looked down at my phone that kept ringing back to back, I wasn't answering it for shit though. Mason, my detail's phone started up next.

"Yeah boss I'm in here. No, he's gone. Ummm-" he started looking me over, confusing the shit outta me. I mean he was looking me over from head to toe. "No, it doesn't look like he touched her. Yes boss, I was on my post outside. Ok gotcha." He sighed handing me the phone.

Fuck, I didn't think about him calling somebody else to get to me. I grabbed the phone out of his hand, pouting like a kid who was caught sneaking food.

"Yes Majik?"

"What the fuck you mean, yes Majik? Why the fuck would you not answer your phone? I'm over here thinking some shit done happened to your stupid ass. Unless yo ass somewhere not breathing, ANSWER YOUR DAMN PHONE."

"I was upset and just didn't wanna talk."

"Bi-" he paused and took a deep breath, I'm guessing to calm himself down. I've never heard him this mad before and I hate I was the cause of it. I know I was in the wrong, so I'm not even gonna trip on the fact his punk ass almost called me a bitch. I'mma let him have that one. "Nautica, why would you think that shit was ok? You can't be out here on some dumb shit. We got muthafuckas coming at us from all sides. Look you need to put in a leave of absence or something!"

"Wait why do I need to do that Majik? What am I supposed to do about money and stuff?"

"Got damn stop asking stupid ass questions! Do what I said man, don't make me come down there and do the shit for you. Oh, and we'll talk about the other bullshit that nigga was speaking on the when I get to the house."

"Whatever you say Majik. It's always what you say!" I didn't give him a chance to say anything back.

I handed the phone back to Mason, grabbed my things and went back to work.

The last few hours of my day were spent being pissed off. All I could think of was the argument we'd had, I was adamant about not putting in a leave of absence. I loved my job and not having to depend on anybody for money. When you give niggas that power, they felt like they could run yo ass.

It was finally time for me to get off and I was happy as shit. I need a shot of the strongest liquor we had. I was walking so fast to the car, I was damn near skipping. Mason was gonna have to break some speeding limits getting me home today.

My face hit the floor when I saw Majik standing outside his

car. I just knew my heart was gonna jump out my chest it was beating so hard.

I had to keep that hard look on my face, I couldn't show him that he intimidated me. I'mma play tough for now, but I'mma cry in the car.

I walked up and stood in front of him not saying a word.

"Nautica why are you trying me shawty?" He had the calmest tone ever and that shit damn near had me ready to run back in the building.

"What are you talking about Majik?"

"Stop playing stupid man, let's go."

I was normally greeted with a kiss and when he didn't do it, I knew he had an issue with me. I went ahead and got in and slammed the door.

He just looked at me and shook his head.

MAJIK

I don't know why this damn girl was trying my patience. I wasn't gonna play into that bullshit she was on. Her ass better get it together and explain to me why I heard that fuck boy say they was married.

When we made it home, her ass has the nerve to be in this muthafucka slamming cabinets and shit.

"Yo, slam another got damn thing in here. In this bitch acting like Majesti, having temper tantrums and shit."

"Majik, what the hell do you want? You been fucking with me all damn day."

"Girl pipe yo ass the fuck down! I ain't did shit to you but try to make sure your ass is safe. Now if you want me to leave your ass out here to fend for yourself, just let me the fuck know."

In the middle of us arguing, I got a text from Majesti saying she wanted me to come pick her up.

My baby girl: Daddy can you come pick me up? I'm ready to come home.

Me: Of course, but what's wrong?

My baby girl: Mommy's new boyfriend is weird daddy.

Me: I'm on the way. Get your stuff ready.

My baby girl: okay daddy

This the stupid shit I be talking about, why the hell would CoCo have some unknown nigga around my got damn daughter? I don't give a shit who she popping her pussy for but do that shit away from Majesti.

"Man read this shit!" I told Nautica handing her my phone.

"What the hell? Come on, why are we still standing here? Let's go get my baby!"

She took off towards the front door, grabbing her purse and putting on her gym shoes that was sitting by the door.

This is why I fuck with her so tough. No matter what we got going on, she always puts my baby girl first and loves her like no other.

"Did you talk to Majesti? Did she sound ok?"

"Nah I didn't talk to her, she just sent the text. She probably doesn't want her crazy ass mama to know she hit me up."

While I was thinking about it, I needed to call that cunt and let her know I was on the way. For the sake of my freedom, I didn't need to be around her any longer than necessary.

The phone rung about five times before she sent me to voicemail. That didn't do anything but piss me off even more. I called again and if she didn't answer, I was going in there guns blazing.

"Yeah, hello."

"Aye, where my daughter at?"

"What you mean where she at? She here with me, in there in her room!"

This hoe must've been tryna impress her nigga, she knew I wasn't with the stupid shit.

"Adjust your tone CoCo, ion know who you tryna impress, but you better drop down a few notches. I'm ten minutes away, have my daughter ready?"

"For what? I'm spending time with her!"

"Who about explain themselves to you? Right plan, wrong man!"

I was done with that conversation and hung up in her face. I was less than ten minutes out, but I wanted to see who she had around my kid. I know CoCo retarded ass will be quick to lie.

I was a second too late cause just as we pulled up, the fuck nigga was pulling out and took off fast as hell down the street.

I blew the horn and Majesti came running out the house like track star and hopped in the back.

"Nautiiiii, I missed you, but I'm soooo mad at you," she said rolling her eyes.

"I missed you too ladybug, but you better fix them eyes. What I tell you about that? You're not grown."

"I'm sorry." She finished just as CoCo made it to my truck.

I already know she was about to be on some bullshit.

"What you coming to get her for?"

I was about to tell her because my daughter called me, but I glanced at Majesti in the rearview mirror and she looked terrified that I was about to rat her out. That didn't sit well with me.

"Cause I missed her that's why, I don't gotta give you a reason to scoop up my child. The real question is, who was that speeding outta here?"

"A friend, why? You got your bitch so don't worry about who I fuck."

"Watch ya mouth before I beat yo ass out here!" Nautica replied calmly.

CoCo knew her ass couldn't fight, so she did what she knew to do best and that was shut the fuck up.

"Get the fuck away from my shit! I'll call you when I'm ready to bring her back. Oh, and another thing, keep niggas out the house I paid for and from around my child." I put the car in drive, so she'd know this conversation was over with.

I'm glad she got the point, backed away, and took her ass back in the house.

I was enjoying just listening to my two ladies carryon a conversation without me. Every time I witnessed their bond, it made me love Nautica that much more.

"So why were you ready to come home ladybug?"

"Oh, my goodness Nauti, my mama's new boyfriend is really weird."

"Who is it and what did he do?" I had to jump in to get the answers I wanted.

"He told me to call him Mr. Dre and I don't know daddy, he kept asking me questions about you and Nautica."

"If you ever see him again, take a picture and send it to me okay baby girl?"

"Yes daddy, can we get something to eat? I'm starving!"

"Yo mama ain't fed you yet?"

She went to roll her eyes, until Nautica caught her, and she changed that tune real quick.

"I ate some cereal this morning, but every time I told her I was hungry, Drae would tell me to go to my room and mama just sat there."

I pulled into Chick Fil A, ordered her something to eat and headed back home. I was gonna make a point to pull up on CoCo tomorrow. The number one thing I don't play with is my daughter.

After watching a few movies and playing a few games with Majesti, it was finally time for her to take her grown ass to sleep. Her ass had the nerve to tell me she had to call Ayanni first. I told Nautica we shouldn't have gotten that damn phone.

I went to my man cave and smoked on some loud, I needed to relieve the stress from today. About an hour after being by myself, I was now ready to deal with the shit from earlier. By Nautica's reaction I knew she had no idea that this fuck boy somehow forged a marriage. I sent Kwame a text to look into this shit, just as he sent me some good info on Solomon. This the shit I've been waiting on. It's about to be go time.

Nauti was just getting out the shower when I walked in the room.

"What you been in here doing?" I'm surprised she didn't jump in the shower as soon as she walked through the door.

"Princess Majesti came in here wanting my attention of course." She laughed.

I just looked at her cause even her laugh was sexy. This girl was everything I needed and wanted, so I'd kill a nigga for her ass.

"So, you ready to talk about today? Before you get all what y'all women say, *in yo feelings*, I'm not mad, but we do need to talk about it?"

I knew she was about to get upset by her demeanor, until I told her ass I wasn't on no bullshit.

"I don't know what you really want me to say Majik. I don't know if it's true, but judging from the paperwork, it looks legit."

"Let me see the shit. I already put Kwame on it to see what he could find out."

She handed me the papers and I could already tell the shit was forged. This wouldn't be hard to fight, but I wasn't gonna go that route. I'm killing his ass, on sight.

"I didn't sign that. How would he have gotten a marriage license without both of us being there?"

"I don't know shawty. I hope that nigga gotta beneficiary cause you bout to be a widow."

"Fuck you punk, that ain't my husband." She threw a pillow at me laughing.

I chilled with my girl for the rest of the night. I'd just got word on where this Solomon nigga was hiding at, so I already know I wasn't gonna be seeing much of them for a few days. These muthafuckas was about to see why they call me crazy. I was bout to release this magic on they ass.

AHNAIS

I was so stressed out trying to plan this wedding. Draiven didn't want to wait so here I was like a damn fool tryna do this shit by myself. I said fuck that shit and hired me a wedding planner. I'mma let her ass be the one stressed the hell out.

Me, my sister, and Nautica had an appointment for me to go find a wedding dress and that had me hype as hell.

I heard Amaris' ignorant ass out there blowing the horn like she ain't have no damn sense.

"Come on Yanni before I have to slap your TeTe."

"So, you mad at me cause TeTe made you mad? Yeah don't make sense to me, but umm okay, I'm coming."

"Not today Yanni, not ta-fucking day!"

"But I-"

"Shut yo' ass up Yanni!" Dravien yelled from the room.

"Leave my damn daughter alone Ahnais. Both y'all get the hell on man, a nigga tryna sleep and shit."

If I didn't have to go, I'd be cussing him out. I paused before I walked out the house cause I for real wanted to cuss this nigga out. Instead, I slammed the door as hard as I could.

"Ooohh mama, daddy gonna get you for that," she said laughing.

"Shut up Yanni and run yo' ass to the car."

Just as we jumped in, Draiven appeared in the doorway with a scowl on his face.

"Drive bitch, don't you see my life in danger!"

Everybody in the car was laughing at my expense. I didn't think the shit was that funny though. I noticed Nautica looking like she had the weight of the world on her shoulders and Amaris wasn't looking any better. I needed to find out what is wrong with these bitches cause they gonna have to get it together on my day.

"Soooo TeTe I heard you knocked up. You do know that I was first right, so that lil baby in your stomach will have to take a backseat to me."

"You do know you ain't my child, right?"

"Ooohh the disrespect!" she said clutching her fake pearls.

"You know TeTe playing Yanni Boo. You'll always be my baby." That's all she needed to hear.

We were so busy catching up on each other's lives, we didn't even realize we had made it already. For some reason I was starting to get butterflies in my stomach. I guess it was all the excitement, cause I know for a fact this is what I wanted to do.

I saw Amaris was by herself looking at bridesmaids' dresses, so it was a good time to see what was on her mind.

"What's wrong sis? Your head ain't here with me." I walked up next to her and asked.

"Oh, it ain't shit. I'm good."

"Girl stop lying to me before we have a problem."

She sighed before saying what she wanted to say.

"Jaysun is driving me crazy. I miss Destiny, so I know he does too, but I can't take his shit. He's being over the fucking top with this baby. Her mother passed during childbirth, so he thinks it's gonna happen to me. Destiny had cancer, so he thinks it's gonna happen to the baby. Bitch do you know this nigga threw all my lil Cuties out? You know how I feel about them lil ass oranges."

This hoe was legit mad.

"Sis don't let it get to you. He loves you and has every right to have his fears. It could be worse, he could be a fuck nigga that don't take care of his responsibilities."

"I guess Chile, but he gonna have to get it together."

Just as I was about to respond to her, we heard a loud voice come in the bridal shop.

"You ugly bitches could have waited on me." My mama came in fussing.

"I told mama to wait on your nana, but she kept saying not ta-day Yanni. Not ta-day." She held her hand up imitating me.

All I could do was roll my eyes at her ole snitching ass.

"Mama, I told you I had an appointment. You decided not to be ready. How'd you get here anyway?"

"Your sour puss ass Fiancé. Oh yeah, he said he beating yo' ass when he gets home tonight. I told him I'll shove an X-acto knife up his ass if he tries it. He gave me $500 to let him do it, so Tina Turner, you're on your own."

"Mama, you sold me out for a measly $500?" That was fucked up.

"You better be ready to eat the cake Anna Mae."

I started walking off shaking my head.

"I can't believe you mama."

"Oh, shut yo' sensitive ass up, I'm about to spend this and still fuck him up. I wasn't about to turn down no money though."

This lady was something else. I started pulling out dresses that caught my eye and trying them on. None of them was making me light up like I was hoping. I still had a few more to go through.

I put the next one on and I immediately fell in love. I literally had tears in my eyes I loved it so much. I stepped out, so I could show everyone and they all had the same reaction. I didn't even wanna try on the last one because this was it for me.

Rubbing my hands down the side, I was thinking about my big day and got sad just that quick.

"Girl that dress is the shit, what's wrong with you?"

"It's not the dress, I love it. I was just thinking, who's gonna walk me down the aisle?"

"How about you let your father have the honor?"

We all turned around to two big ass Italian men standing behind us, dripping with money.

"Nigga I wish the fuck you would even try, you lying community dick muthafucka!"

"Mama who is that?"

"Your hoe ass sperm donor!" It was apparent my mama was mad as fuck.

I couldn't get to my phone, so I looked at Nautica with my eyes, looking down at her phone, and hoping she'd get the hint.

I didn't know this man and if it's between my man and my brothers, I'mma always choose my family.

"I see you still got a smart-ass mouth Frankie," he laughed and looked her up and down, I guess admiring what he saw. "You still fine as hell too."

"Fuck you! Why are you here?"

"I wanted a chance to get to know my girls."

"That ain't gonna happen!" My mama answered before either one of us could.

I looked at Amaris cause I noticed she hadn't really said anything since this man been in here.

"Look girls, there's a lot I need to say to you both. Let's have lunch and just give me a chance to let you know everything. Here's my number, just call me when you're ready."

With that he was gone just as quick as he came and thirty seconds later, two of our details came busting through the door. They pick a fine fucking time to be coming to our rescue. We coulda been good and dead by now.

Five minutes after our detail came in the guys came. I'm glad I had sense enough to hurry and get out of my dress. I had a feeling they were gonna be coming. Especially after Nautica let us know she was able to send Majik a message.

I know these people thought we were ghetto ass hell, up in here in the good establishment with this bullshit.

"Y'all done?"

"Yeah, I found a dress I love, so we're all set. The girls just gotta find their bridesmaids dress next weekend."

"What's the price so we can get the fuck up outta here shawty?"

"Ummm excuse me ma'am." I had to get the worker's attention. Them lil white ladies got the hell outta dodge with the quickness. She finally came over, looking scared and timid. "What's the price of the gown I settled on?" This is my fiancé and he's gonna pay for it now."

I had to make sure I slid that in, so she didn't mess around and bring the dress in here for him to see.

"Okay, let's see, it'll be ummm $4,997." This bitch looked at us with her eyebrow raised like we were just in here to play dress up and dream.

"You sure that's all you need and it's the one you really want?" he asked as he handed her his black card.

Her demeanor changed once she saw we weren't broke ghetto black folks. I shook my head at him and waited for the receipt. The worker that originally helped me came from the back to make sure I was all set.

"Y'all need to head on back to the house if y'all done," Draiven told us. I was sick of having to be cooped up in the house.

"No, I'm tired of having to be stuck in the house all the time. If we aren't working we're expected to be home. This is my day and I want to damn enjoy it."

"What else do you have to do Nais?"

"We were going to have lunch." I made sure to give him attitude, so he would know I was irritated.

"Man hold on!"

He got on his phone and made a couple of calls. These fools were in the parking lot with guns pulled out waiting for some just in case shit.

"Listen, we got a few more niggas coming to detail ya'll. The niggas from today not gonna be able to do it anymore. So, let me know what the move is after ya'll finish eating. We got some shit to handle so I can't be your security."

"Whatever Draiven, as long as I can do what I want to do. Ya'll need to handle whatever ya'll need to because I am sick of having people babysit me."

"Worry about what you need to worry about, nothing else."

We stood around and chit chatted for a few until the new detail crew came. I don't even want to think about what's going to happen to them fools that was supposed to be watching us.

We finally made it to the Old Lady Gang restaurant and the first person we saw when walking in was Kandi's husband Todd. Her auntie Nora was walking around from table to table greeting everyone. I thought that was super dope, she making people feel at home.

Nautica was heading to the restroom, so that was the perfect time to see what was up with her. I let her go first and after a minute or so, I went in behind her. Waiting at the sink for her to come out the stall, I posted up like I was waiting to confront her about some fuck shit. She jumped when she came out and saw me standing there.

"Hoe, you scared the shit out of me. Why in the hell are you standing there not saying shit?"

"I need to ask you something. Why you been looking crazy all day? You and Amaris' asses been blowing my happy high today."

"Girl my bad, but if you only knew."

"I'm trying to now so spill the beans."

"Draego popped up at my job the other day. He showed me some paperwork that stated we were legally married. I don't know how he made that happen, because I would have never willingly married him."

"Damnnnnn, what the hell you gonna do?"

"Of course, Majik said he was gonna take care of it. I've never wished death on nobody, but I for real wish he'd die."

"Hoe, you know Majik is gonna make that happen. Stop worrying about that shit."

"Yeah, I guess." She shrugged her shoulders and let out a long sigh.

After she washed her hands, we went back out to join everyone else.

Just as I walked back up to the table, I was approached by someone that looked very familiar.

"I guess this is fate being as though we just keep running into each other."

"Do I know you?"

"Damn now my feelings are hurt. I thought for sure I left a lasting impression on you."

"Didn't I tell you my daddy didn't like people talking to my mommy? You're a lil thirsty ain't you?" Of course, little Ms. Yanni had to put in her two cents, but then it clicked where I saw this guy at.

I'm starting to wonder why in the hell this man keeps popping up everywhere I'm at. I know I'm exaggerating, but still. I just saw him at the mall not too long ago, that shit is scary as hell.

"I'm sorry Ms. Lady, I just saw something that I like."

"Well go see something else!" she said turning up her nose.

"Shit, I'll take you. You a fine piece of something walking around here."

I couldn't even respond, because before I could say something T.C and Mason, two of our details came walking up. Them buff ass niggas didn't even give the man a chance to explain why he was talking to me. They immediately escorted him away from us. The rest of our lunch date went well without any more interruptions. We were able to cut the hell up and enjoy ourselves without worrying about a damn thing. That's the kind of outings I love and look forward to many more. I'll be glad as fuck when they handle all the bullshit.

AMARIS

This pregnancy was already giving me hell. I couldn't stop throwing up for shit. No matter what I put in my mouth, it came right back up. Not only do I have to deal with feeling fucked up, Jaysun's ass was on some good bullshit. I only told Ahnais half of the shit I was dealing with. This nigga was starting to come in the house later and later. Sometimes he'd come in smelling like perfume, I know good and damn well I don't wear the cheap shit he been smelling like.

He done linked up with Majik and them on some other shit, so his time out in the streets been even crazier. I know one thing though, if I find out this nigga out here slinging his dick, I'mma end up in jail.

We were getting low on groceries, so I was spending my Sunday at the store. I had so much shit in the cart it didn't make no sense. I knew half of this stuff, Jaysun was gonna more than likely throw away. I only got away with eating what I want when my mom or his was over at the house.

I started looking around cause I felt like somebody was watching me. Looking to my left, I came face to face with some big face bitch with her nose turned up at me. The bitch was pushing her cart in my direction just as my phone rung.

"Hello."

"What's up girl, what you on today?" Nautica asked smacking in my ear. That was so got damn annoying.

"Shit, at the grocery store right now, about to slap a bitch," I said starting at this hoe dead in her face.

"Bitch send me yo location," I heard her shuffling around.

"Girl calm your extra violent ass down; these hoes out here don't really want no smoke. They play tough."

"Shit, what's the beef? Who is the bitch?"

"Girl I don't know, some off-brand bitch that's staring at me in this store like she knows me and wanna eat my pussy."

The lil staring hoe finally made it all the way past me and just like I figured, she just kept staring and didn't say shit. That put me on alert cause hoes don't act like that unless they fucking your nigga. I wasn't gonna confront shawty though, that would make me look insecure as fuck.

"Ewwwww, as long as you good though. What else up? This my last day off work and I wanna do something."

"What you tryna do boo?" I questioned as I put the last few items I needed in the cart.

I made my way towards the checkout counter, so I could get my big pregnant ass up outta there. It seemed like that bitch wanted me to see her ass cause she was right in the next line still watching me.

"I don't know man, let's cookout or something today. It's gonna be getting cool soon and I wanna take advantage of this nice weather."

"Is Ahnais off today?"

"No, she'll be getting off in an hour though."

"I'm down, I don't know what the fuck Jaysun got going on, but I'll let him know." The unknown hoe walked passed me and giggled when I mentioned not knowing what Jaysun had going on. "What time are you talking about? I'm just leaving the store and I'm not about to shop again for meat, so I'll just bring something I just got."

"Aight come through around three p.m. and we can turn the fuck up." She hung up as I walked to my car keeping my eye on that lil hoe.

I could have confronted the lil raggedy slut bucket, but what is the point? I ain't fucking this bitch and we ain't in a relationship. I made sure to get a good picture of her ass though, I wanted proof.

I didn't even bother calling Jaysun to let him know that we were cooking out at Nautica's. Shit, I wouldn't care if his ass starved at this point. I don't like to be the girlfriend to be accusing her man of shit, but hell the signs are right there.

I saw my detail behind me and I really wanted to shake his ass and run the hell away. I got a man claiming to be my father that I haven't ever seen in my damn life and I got the man that's supposed to love me cheating possibly. Not to mention I'm pregnant by his ass. I swear that's some fuck shit.

Ahnais doesn't wanna have anything to do with this Solomon character, but I really wanna know why he left us. I have questions that I want answered. I copied the number from the card he handed my sister, I'm just waiting on the perfect time to call.

The BBQ...

I'm so glad Nautica suggested having this BBQ, shit was lit as fuck and just what I needed to clear my mind. Majik had so much food on the grill and my big greedy ass couldn't wait until I could smash it.

I walked over to him to see if it was a hot dog ready that I could steal. Seeing all that food was making me drool.

"Brooothhhherrr!" I whined and walked up to Majik on the grill.

"What sis? Don't come fucking with me. I gotta show Draiven's non-grilling ass how it's done. Don't mess up my concentration."

"I'm hungry Majik, come on please? Just give me one of them hot dogs."

"Here ole fat ass girl." He grabbed a napkin and put me two good burnt hot dogs on it.

"Nigga don't be talking about my girl," Jaysun said walking up behind me.

I did the dramatic eye roll. I mean eyeballs so far up, them muthafuckas like to got stuck.

"Fuck you nigga." They laughed and dapped it up.

"Bring ya ass here Amaris," he said walking away. Like I was a puppy and about to follow his ass. Yeah, he had me fucked up about four ways.

"Make sure you holla at me bout that before you leave," Majik demanded whispering in my ear.

I shook my head cause I knew Majik was gonna pick up on my attitude. His ass doesn't miss shit and being he always played the big brother roll, I already know he was gonna grill the hell up outta me.

"Amaris!" he called out, I guess he realized I wasn't following him. This man was looking at me like I'd grown six heads. I'd never acted this way towards him, so I know I had him tripping.

"Go on and handle that sis, don't give these muthafuckas a show."

I guess Majik was right, so I headed in the direction of my hoe ass baby daddy. We found a spare bedroom and walked in. I sat my oversized ass on the bed, crossed my legs and my arms and waited for him to say whatever it was he wanted to get off his chest.

"What bullshit you on shawty?"

I played mute like I didn't hear him, just like he didn't know where home was. Niggas kill me doing stupid shit, but act like we do the most. He walked up on me like he wanted these problems. I know Majik had a pistol somewhere in this room, I'd light his ass up like the fourth of July.

He kept calling my name and after the fifth or sixth time, I got tired of hearing it over and damn over.

"Why the hell you keep calling my name like I'm not sitting here?" I made sure to give him as much attitude as possible.

"Ma, I swear you bout to make me beat your ass in here!"

Just then somebody quickly opened the door.

"Put ya hands on ha, come on I wanna see ya do it!" my mama came in waving a gun jumping around like she was really Madea. Her ass nosey as shit. The fact that the shit was so funny, I couldn't even say anything to her for bussing up in here.

"I apologize Ms. Frankie, we good in here. You know I'd never hurt her. Can I get a few more minutes with Amaris, so we can come back and enjoy the BBQ?"

"You charming muthafucka you," she said walking back out and closing the door behind her.

"Why are acting like this ma?"

"You cheating on me Jaysun?" I might as well get right to the point.

"Girl what the fuck are you speaking on? Ain't nobody cheating on you!"

"Alright, that's all I need to know, we good."

I got up and walked out the room. We didn't have shit else to talk about at the moment. I asked him, and he said no, if or when I find out otherwise, shit ain't gonna look too good for his ass. I gave him an opportunity to be honest, now whether he is or not, I'll find out soon enough.

"You good cousin?" Nautica came up looking concerned.

"You know your crazy ass mama came out here going off and shit." She laughed, I did too cause I know she was being extra.

After about an hour, all the food was done, and people was scattering to the plates like roaches. I didn't even know who some of these hoes was, but if they knew what was good for them, they'd fall the hell back. I'm big, pregnant, irritated, hot and hungry. These rat face bitches don't have no kinda home training.

I pushed my way through the line and dared one of them to jump stupid and I be damned if one of them didn't.

"Ummm excuse me, you can get in line just like everybody else. Your fat ass is rude. I slap bitches, pregnant and all."

I took a minute to gather myself cause I was about to slap her ass and I needed all my strength. I wasn't lying when I said it was hot as shit out here and I got tired easily.

"Excuse me sir, but do your mother have a black dress?" Of course, my little ride or die Yanni had to add her two cents.

"I am a woman little girl and what does that have to do with anything?" she was for real a dumb one if she didn't even understand a child was threatening her life.

"Oh, I'm truly sorry Sir/Ma'am, you look like a whole dude out here. That mustache is enough to fool anybody, but anyway, I just want to make sure your mom has something to bury you in. You can't be talking to my TeTe like you're crazy Sir!"

"Shut up Yanni!" everyone yelled at the same time, but of course it was laughter while it was said. I dare not tell my baby to be quiet at a time like this.

"You don't want it with her ma!" one of the guys that worked for the fellas shouted out.

"Fuck her!"

See, I tried to give her a pass, but little Miss-talk-a-lot just couldn't close her mouth. I gave her the three piece she was busting her ass to get. I was even nice enough to give it to her in the mouth. Her ass took off running with a mouth full of blood and I hope this was an example to any of these basic bitches that thought they wanted to try me today.

"Are you really out here fighting with my got damn baby in your stomach?"

"I wasn't fighting, I hit the bitch and she ran off bleeding."

Everyone had gone back to minding their business and trying to eat. Jaysun shook his head and walked off, I'm assuming pissed off.

The people that was already in line let me in front, I guess they didn't wanna feel the wrath of the hungry pregnant lady. I fixed me two big plates because I didn't wanna have to get up and get another one. I doubt I'd eat all this food, but you never know.

We all was enjoying our time eating good, laughing and joking, playing cards, and just relaxing for once. Nobody was acting stupid or on any bullshit, other than the bitch that had to get punch in the face. I enjoyed being around shit like this. I guess Jaysun had let go of his attitude because he was back stuck up under me.

The guys were talking shit over a game of spades when all of a sudden, they all jumped up with guns in their hands, pushing us back behind them.

"Nigga you got a death wish coming to my crib!" Majik barked out mad as shit. "Majesti, you and the kids go in the house NOW!" they took off running inside.

Draego was here, but what was shocking was the fact that CoCo was with him. How in the hell did these two idiots meet? Yanni ran by and I notice that nigga looking at her hard and strange. It was almost like a lightbulb went off in his demented mind.

"Bitch you got some fucking nerves popping up over here and with this nigga at that!"

"What's wrong with you now? This is my boyfriend Drae, I didn't come to cause any problems. I didn't even know ya'll had company. I wanted to take Majesti out for the day and Majik wasn't answering his phone."

I was concerned about my sister and looking over at her, it looked like she was about to have an anxiety attack.

"Damn, this how my lovely wife living?

"Your wife? What are you talking about?" CoCo asked dumbfounded looking at Draego for a response.

He just gave her the death stare and she shut her ass right the fuck up.

"You got about five seconds to tell me what you doing at my house before you make the Channel 5 news!"

I walked over to Ahnais and sat her down while Nautica gave her a bottle of water and Selina gave her a paper towel.

"Damn Nautica, I should have come down to Atlanta with

you a long time ago, you got some fine ass family members." He licked his lips eyeing each one of us. The fellas cocked their guns at the same time. "Ok, ok look, we just came to get her daughter. I ain't come for no trouble boss." He played with the toothpick in his mouth and smirked.

I knew this muthafucka was on some funny shit by that gesture alone. I didn't like the fact he knew where Nautica laid her head, which fucking with that bird brain ass bitch, he probably already knew.

"Well my daughter ain't going nowhere with ya'll, so you and this bitch can get the fuck up outta here."

"Majik, you can't keep me from my daughter. I have the right to get her, I do have custody of her or did you forget?"

"Nah bitch, did you? You ain't been thinking about my fucking daughter. Oh, you didn't get the court ordered papers for you to be in court last week? By the look on your face you didn't, but let me bring you up to speed, I have legal full custody of Majesti now and like I said, she ain't going no got damn where. Now for the last time get the fuck up outta here."

"You're wrong for that Majik and you will get what's coming to you."

"Man, she wants her daughter, so you gonna need to hand her over."

POW

Before we knew it, Majik gave Draego a leg shot. I wish he'd shot his ass in the damn head. I'm sure the only reason he didn't was the fact that the kids were in the house. I know they couldn't hear the shot, because of the silencer, but that shit would have been crazy if one of them would have walked out here and a dead man was laying in front of them.

That nigga dropped to the floor quick as hell and all dramatic.

"What you will never in your life do is tell me what the fuck to do concerning my got damn daughter. The only reason you getting to live right now is because of that little girl in there. I don't kill where she lay her head at, but don't make me change my mind," Majik warned him with the pistol to his head.

"Okay Majik, we're going. Can you please have Majesti call me tonight?"

"Bitch get this hoe ass nigga and get the fuck up outta my face. I'll think about it."

CoCo helped him up and they went on about their business. The guys sent some of their workers to make sure shit was good and they actually had left. They had let security come to the back to get something to eat which wasn't the best decision if you ask me. That's how they were able to get to the back. Anybody could have come at us, luckily it was just CoCo this time.

They know what the hell they're up against, shit like this can't be happening. I'm sure they were thinking the same thing, judging by the looks on all of their faces. We were enjoying ourselves too, it's always that one person that gotta ruin the damn fun. I knew this shit wasn't gonna be over until they killed Draego's ass.

DRAIVEN

That shit that happened at Malik's spot the other day was crazy as hell. I wanted so bad to put a bullet into that nigga head. I know my boy wanted to get at Draego for the shit he did to Nautica, but he gonna have to pass his ass off. I think what he did to my girl was way worse. I saw the way he looked at Yanni and that didn't sit too well with me. I don't know if he was looking at her because he was planning on doing something to her or he realized she looked familiar to his rapist ass.

Right after this wedding we had one last meeting with Marcelo and we will officially be the Connects. I'd been out a little more than normal and Ahnais has already been complaining, so I was hoping she'd be able to handle this new transition we were about to go through. She on that bullshit thinking a nigga cheating on her ass, but I ain't never willingly cheated on my girl.

I got an unexpected call today and the shit threw me for a loop. I couldn't believe this nigga had the audacity to be hitting me up asking to meet up. Of course, I had to hit up the fellas to let them know what was going on, they didn't think it was a good idea for me to take this meeting, but a nigga like me was savage as fuck. I didn't give a fuck about the what ifs.

I was almost at Agave, a restaurant this meeting was taking place at. My ass was running a little behind cause I was trying to get me a little pussy. If this was going to be my last day living, I wanted to make sure I went out with my nuts good and empty and my girl greatly satisfied.

When I pulled up, I checked to make sure my clip was fully loaded and one already in the chamber. I walked in that bitch like I ran it and feared nothing. I bypassed the hostess and made my way straight to my awaiting guest.

"I'm glad you could join me Draiven."

"Don't be glad yet, what the fuck you want with me?"

"It was brought to my attention that you and your people were looking for me."

That muthafucka sat back and put a cigar in his mouth like he just knew for a fact that his ass was safe.

"Naw muthafucka, I believe it's the other way around. You came fucking with me and my brothers. You fuck with us, we fuck with you," I told Solomon's ass.

"You see that's where you have it wrong. I have no need to disturb you and your business, but you my friend have been causing a lot of trouble for my people."

"So, what we about to sit here and play gameshow gangsta?

Say what the fuck you brought me here to say man, I got shit to do."

"Wha-"

"Nigga yo ass don't listen for shit man. Fuck is you doing here bruh?" I looked behind me and Majik and Lenyx was walking up talking shit with a hard ass mug on their faces.

I didn't expect nothing less of their asses. It didn't surprise me that they showed up here, it would have surprised me if they didn't show up.

"Glad that you could join us Mr. Alexander, please have a seat." Here this nigga goes puffing that damn cigar.

"Muthafucka I don't take orders from you, but what you can do is tell me what kinda bullshit you on? You gotta know a nigga want yo life!"

"I don't take to kindly to threats young man. Now out of respect for the simple fact we've both been duped, I haven't killed you. Watch your fuckin tone with me."

"Fuck yo-"

"Majik come on bro, chill out." I stood up to get in between the two of them. I already know my bro was on some ready to kill type shit, especially since we been looking for this nigga for weeks. I needed to know what the point of this visit was before he blew his head off. "Keep your cool bruh, we need to see what this muthafucka want. He called for a reason, like he said, he could've killed me the minute I walked in this bitch if he really wanted to," I whispered trying to talk some sense into him.

He didn't say shit, but the look he gave me and Lenyx when he sat down at the table wasn't a good one. He wanted to kill somebody, and his hostile ass was mad as fuck he didn't have an opportunity.

"So, what's the point of this shit here?" Lenyx sat back and asked. These niggas couldn't be civil for nothing.

Solomon looked at the both of them with a stern look on his face, I could tell he wanted to go off, but he held his composure.

"Word got back to me that you and your people had been looking for me and it was a price on my head. It threw me for a loop and I was baffled because I tend to stay in my own lane."

Now it was my turn to interrupt his ass cause this nigga and his camp been coming at us for a minute now.

"This is where I gotta stop you. You and your people came at us out of nowhere and even approached my muthafuckin seed. On that shit alone, I shoulda ended your shit the minute I walked in this bitch, but just out of curiosity I wanted to hear what the fuck you had to say, but the one thing I ain't gonna do is let you play with my intelligence."

"I'm usually not the type of man to explain myself, but this is a different circumstance. I'm trying to rebuild a relationship with my daughters and killing their family wouldn't help me in any way. I'm being set up by somebody in my camp."

"So, you expect us to believe that shit? You appear in town and all of a sudden we getting shot at, bitches working for you in our shit dropping your name, and muthafuckas approaching my child, nah some shit ain't adding up." I sat back in my chair awaiting his response. Flagging down the waitress, I ordered a shot of Cîroc.

I looked over at bruh and he was deep in thought. I couldn't wait to hear what he thought about this shit. We all equally ran shit, but each one of us had our own unique qualities and Majik was the thinker. He was able to go off his gut instinct on certain situations and nine out ten times he was right. The only person that was able to fool him was his baby mama and he still kicking himself in the ass for that one.

"So, if it ain't you then who is it?"

"I don't know who I can or can't trust right now, I haven't figured it out yet. My father died a little over a year ago and I inherited everything. Somebody is out to get me, that I do know for sure."

"You don't have too long to figure it out. What I do know is this, a muthafucka don't have no more chances to get close to my family."

"You can believe what you want. I just want to get to know my children, but I tell you what if you kill me you better make sure I'm dead." His Italian accent was on full display at this point.

He grabbed his hat, put out his cigar, and got up and left. This shit was even more confusing than when I first got here.

I paid the waitress for my drink and we got the fuck up outta there. When I walked outside, I saw truckloads of niggas on go. This fool done brought an army. What the hell he thought we was about to do, have a gunfight in broad daylight in a busy parking lot?

"You on your John Wayne shit today huh? Nigga is you tryna go to jail? Let's get the fuck up outta here, I'll meet y'all niggas at the spot."

I jumped my ass in my ride and sparked up the fattest spliff. This is why my ass smoked so damn much, it's always some shit going on. I just wanted to get this money, keep my lady and kids happy, and stay out the way of bullshit. What the fuck was so damn hard about that? These fools made it there before me and I already knew they was about to get on my got damn nerves.

"Nigga what the fuck kinda shit your ass on man?" got damn Lenyx didn't even give the door a chance to close before he started with the damn lectures.

"Muthafucka shut you yo ass up, I don't need no fucking babysitter. I made a choice to do some shit and I did it, end of fucking discussion."

"Yeah aight, yo dumb ass coulda been walking into a fucking trap."

"So, you wanna sit around here and argue like we a fucking couple or figure out what the fuck is really going on?"

I was really getting tired of the got damn lecturing and shit like I wasn't a grown ass man. I do what the fuck I wanna do, when I wanna fucking do it.

"What the hell you mean figure it out? We already know what the hell going on and we shoulda killed that fucking Italian while we had the chance."

"So, you mean to tell me that none of the shit that nigga said made sense?"

"Do old women look good in bikinis? Hell naw!"

"I wish ya'll bitches would shut the fuck up. A nigga can't even think with ya'll arguing like a bunch of females."

"NIGGA FUCK YOUU!" me and Lenyx both said while looking at Majik like he was fucking retarded or something.

"We need to look into this shit a little deeper, something ain't adding up. Why would this man come to us twice and not do shit? He had two fucking chances and ain't did shit."

"Man put Kwame on the shit, I'm bout to go home and get me some pussy." This fool got up and walked towards the door. "Oh yeah, some nigga hit me up about doing business. He said that nigga Dolo gave him my information. I'mma check his ass out and that nigga Dolo need to get handled. He out here running his fucking mouth like a got damn bitch, that's how niggas get caught up with the law."

Once them niggas was gone, I was left to sort out these bricks that needed to be handed out in the morning. We all had our days to do this shit and unfortunately for me, today was mine. I didn't really have to do shit but make sure these muthafuckas in this bitch had the weight and the count right, so until they were done doing what the hell they had to do, I just chilled in the office watching the monitors and ESPN.

COCO

If I knew what type of nigga this really was before I got with him, I would have run the other way. I should have known something was up with him the way he kept asking me questions about my baby daddy and his bitch. Ever since he got shot at Majik's house that day, he's been beating my ass like I was a field nigga. He switched up so damn quick I didn't see it coming. He got this big elaborate scheme to take down Majik and Nautica, I'm all for that as long as my baby isn't involved. I may not be the best mother, but I wouldn't allow her to be in harm's way.

"CoCo where the fuck is my got damn pain medicine at?" Draego asked limping in the living room.

"Ummm I put them up, I didn't think you needed them since you had drunk that alcohol."

"Bitch did I muthafuckin ask you what the fuck you

thought?" He smacked so much fire out of me I coulda had a whole campfire right here.

"What I do this time Drae?" I looked up at him holding my face crying and asked.

I wondered if I let Majik know what I was going through, if he would even care enough to help me. He would probably lose his damn mind if he knew this man was living in the house he bought. I'm pretty sure he wouldn't waste any time putting me out this muthafucka. I was having mixed feelings going along with the shit this crazy ass man had planned. I really just didn't know what to do.

He'd hooked up with some people that wanted Majik and the guys out the way, I don't know how the hell he even met them in the first place. I tried not to ask too many questions though, the less I knew the better off I'd be.

"CoCo go get my shit before I beat your ass man, for real."

I don't know how much his crimpled ass thought he would be able to do, but for the sake of not getting smacked again, I just went and got it.

My phone started ringing and I didn't even get to look at the screen good before it was snatched out of my hand. He looked at it and threw it back at me. Once I picked it up and noticed it was my best friend, I really didn't want to answer. After all, she was the one telling me that something didn't seem to right about Drae and to watch out for him. Me wanting a man in my life that damn bad, I didn't listen. The way he was looking at me, I knew I needed to go ahead and take the call, so he didn't think I was up to some funny shit.

"Hello!"

"Hey girl, what's up with your ass? You got a new nigga and can't call a bitch now, what's up with that?" Kaycie asked smacking in my ear as usual.

"Nah, you know it's never like that." I sighed, I wanted so bad to be able to let her know what the fuck was going on.

"Damn bitch, what's wrong with you? You sound sad as fuck. It's time for us to go out and turn the fuck up."

The whole time I was on the phone, this nigga was giving me the I wish you would look. He was for real all up in my damn mouth. I couldn't send out a bat signal if I wanted to. I stayed on the line with Kaycie for about five more minutes and I had to get off. I couldn't take the stare down any longer.

I was just about to go climb in the bed and catch up on my reality shows when the doorbell rang, and I damn near shitted on myself. I didn't know if it was Majik at the door and I couldn't tell you who I was scared of more at the moment, him or Draego. Since it was my damn house, I went to see who was at the door, but was stopped in my tracks.

"Man sit yo ass the fuck down, ain't nobody here for your ass!"

Well excused the fuck outta me, I mean this is my shit, well technically not my shit, but still. I made like I was going in the room but stayed in the hallway, so I could be nosey. I heard him in there talking to some young man that looked and sounded Italian. After I heard them ending their conversation and the door open back up, I tried to hurry up and run in the room.

"Aye so look, the shit we talked about is going down tomorrow. My homie got everything set up for us," Draego said limping in the room.

"I'm still confused as to why I have to drag my child into this shit."

"Look she is that niggas weakness. If we can throw him off his square, it'll be easier to get at him. Just be fucking ready and don't fuck up.

The next day...

I was nervous as hell walking into Majesti's day camp. I had no idea if they'd taken my name off the pick-up list or not.

"Hi, can I help you?"

"Yes, I'm here to pick up Majesti Alexander." I was praying this lady couldn't see my chest beating fast as hell. I felt like I was about to pass out I was so fucking scared.

"Your name please?" she asked checking something on the computer screen. After I told her my name and showed her my I.D, she handed it back and called for someone to bring Majesti up.

I was surprised like hell that that muthafucka hadn't gone as far as to take my name off the list. This bitch made sure to point out that she'd only seen Nautica pick up my daughter. I was almost in the clear when some airhead hoe had to come up and open her mouth.

"Hi, you're here to pick up Majesti? I thought her stepmom was getting her early today for a doctor's appointment?"

"Yeah, she was, but I told her I was already out. I'm her mother, listen we have to go, is MY child on the way up?"

I was getting sick and tired of these bitches referencing Nautica like she mattered to me. The only person that gave a fuck about that bitch is my stupid ass baby daddy. Well it seems like that's Draego's problem, but he swears it's because Majik shot him. Only time will tell, I guess.

Majesti finally made it up to the front and the look she gave me almost gave me away. She looked at me like I was the scum of the damn earth, like her ass didn't come up outta my pussy.

"Why are you here picking me up?" her smart mouth ass asked me. She didn't even have the decency to give me a damn hello first.

"Hey baby girl, mommy is here to take you to the doctor." I gave these folks the fakest mama voice I could muster up.

"You ain't never ta-"

"Come on Majesti before we're late." I stopped her from finishing her sentence and rushed her lil ass out the building.

I didn't have time to be going back and forth with this got damn child. I didn't have the patience to deal with her smart-ass mouth for too long, so whatever plan this man had needed to go quick as hell.

Once we made it to the car, I could see the sinister look on his face and I immediately knew I had fucked up and made the wrong choice yet again.

Lord protect me and my daughter.

LENYX

*S*hit been in an uproar for days now. Majik has been tearing shit up since my niece been missing. I don't know what CoCo was thinking by taking Majesti, but her ass was as good as dead. It wasn't shit nobody would be able to do to keep that nigga from putting her to sleep.

Draiven and I been holding it down on the business end while he handles shit with the family.

My phone was blowing up and if I didn't want to miss any calls that may be concerning my niece, I would've ignored it. I looked at the screen and noticed it was Selina. I thought I'd found a good girl for once, but she been really acting weird since Majesti been missing. What I do know though is she better not be on some bullshit or her ass will end up on a missing person's poster next to Tori. In the meantime, I was just going to have to go with the flow of things. I'mma die fucking random hoes if this shit doesn't work out with this chick.

"What up?" I answered trying not to give off too much emotion.

"Hey umm umm what's umm going on?"

"Got damn girl spit it out. You been on some funny acting shit man, is it something you need to tell me?" It wasn't no use in beating around the bush.

"Can you meet me for lunch Lenyx? I know you're busy, but this won't take long."

She had my mind wondering now. Even if I didn't have time, I was gonna find it.

"Meet me at the bar on the corner of Providence and MLK. I'm on the way."

I jumped in my 2018 Chrysler 300s and headed towards the bar. Since I had so much shit on my damn mind, I rode with my Glock close by and ready. All a nigga had to do was say the wrong shit and he was gonna be maggot food. I'd gotten there earlier than Selina and that's just how I wanted it. I needed to be able to watch her every move until I can trust her. I made her wait about ten or fifteen minutes before I joined her. The moment I walked up on her and saw her face, I almost forgot that her ass was suspect. She was so damn beautiful, and her ditzy personality made her perfect in my eyes.

"So, what's up? Talk!" We might as well go ahead and get straight to the shit.

"Why are you being so mean and rude to me Lenyx?" she looked like she was on the verge of crying.

She almost had a nigga, but I had to hold it together.

"Mannnnn, ain't nobody being mean to your ass. You wanted to talk, so I'm saying talk."

"I think I may know who got beef with ya'll," she stopped what she was saying and looked at me.

"Go head!"

She rolled her eyes at me, but I didn't give a fuck about her attitude at this point. I feel like this the same shit with Tori all over again, can't trust her ass.

"I was at my cousin Bianca's house the other day and her boyfriend Luca and his friends were over. They were talking about this scheme they had going with somebody to take ya'll down." She paused for a second, I didn't know if it was because her fucking ass was guilty of some shit or just nervous. Either way, I was about to find out. I didn't give a shit about who was in this bar. I pulled out my nine and laid it on the table. This bitch was bout to stop playing with me. "I never told her who I was dating, so I stayed and listened. They were drunk and talking shit."

"So how long you been knowing this shit? Why you just now opening your mouth about it? I been with you damn near every day and if I wasn't with you, I've talked to you."

"I didn't know how to tell you, look at how you're acting now. You constantly compare things I do to Tori, I didn't want or need you comparing this situation to what that bitch did to you."

"Yeah whatever man, what's them niggas names?"

"Luca and Angelo Baressi, I do know they're cousins. Bianca talks just about as much as they do."

"I'm confused, I thought their racist ass family didn't allow them to date outside of their race?"

"That was when the head of the family was still living. He died recently. That's really all I know."

I don't know how to feel about Selina right now, I'mma need a minute to digest all this shit. Only thing good that came out of this is she gave me more info than I had before.

"'Preciate the info shawty, I'mma holla at you later." I started to get up and she stopped me looking sad and shit.

"That's it Lenyx, we aren't gonna talk about us?"

"On the real shawty, I can't even focus on that shit right now. My niece is missing, and we got muthafuckas out here coming for us for reasons we still don't fucking know. I don't know what to believe right now."

"I'm not trying to set you up Lenyx, you know that!"

"You can lower yo muthafucka voice box while you talking to me and I don't know shit!"

I had shit I needed to be doing and sitting here going back and forth with this damn girl wasn't gonna get it done. I started to have some feelings for shawty I can't even lie, but I refused to get made a fool of again. My intentions wasn't to try to hurt her feelings, but mine were more important at the moment.

"Listen, let me figure some shit out and see what the hell going on. I'm not saying we can't work on shit with us, but I need a minute to see what's up."

She was getting to me with them fucking tears rolling down her face and sniffing bullshit. I chopped it up with her for a few more minutes and made sure she was straight before I got the fuck outta dodge.

My next stop was to pop up on Kwame ass. He was about two seconds from getting a bullet right between the eyes. We pay him good got damn money and the nigga ain't finding out shit. It's about time for us to revamp a lot of shit, especially when we take over or Marcelo.

Ain't no damn way niggas should have one up on us like this and muthafuckas damn sure shouldn't have been able to get Majesti like that. I don't give a damn if it was her whack ass mammy. If word get out one person was able to one up us, niggas all over will start trying that shit.

I pulled out my phone to call Draiven, I didn't want his aggravating ass talking shit cause I hadn't made it back to the warehouse. Technically I was fucking working though.

"Fam I swear you sorry as shit, muthafucka don't never wanna do no got damn work."

"Damn nigga shut yo hoe ass up sometimes. All you do is talk shit, I'm starting to wonder bout yo ass."

"Kiss my ass with all that bullshit you talking man, we got shit to. Fuck yo ass at bruh?"

"If you shut the fuck up I'll tell you what the hell I'm on, got damn." He finally closed his mouth long enough for me to talk. "I'm headed to check this nigga Kwame. This muthafucka ain't working efficient enough for me man."

"Well fuck, we on the same shit. I'm headed that way too. I'm bout five minutes away."

"That's a bet, I got some something I need to rap to you

about first though, so wait for me before you holla at him. I'm not too far, it'll take me about ten minutes."

"Aight nigga bet."

We hung up at the same time and I put a little pep in my step. I was trying to get there around the same time his ass did. That nigga wasn't the type to follow directions, he'd run in there and beat the shit outta Kwame off GP.

When I pulled up, surprisingly he was standing outside his car waiting. It sounded like he was on the phone arguing with sis, so I stood back for a few until he handled that. I wasn't about to stand in his face and listen to his family affairs.

"That got damn woman be on some bullshit sometimes bruh!" he sighed sounding frustrated after he'd hung up with Ahnais. "So, what up? It sounded like you had some shit to say my nigga."

"Bruh, you think you got problems? Check this shit out. Went to meet up with Selina's ass and she hit me with some shit about overhearing two niggas plotting on us. Some muthafuckas by the name of Luca and Angelo. They supposed to be cousins or some bullshit like that. They related to that nigga Solomon somehow."

"So that nigga was lying to us and how the hell she knows this shit? Don't tell me her ass the opps, we gotta kill her ass too? Why the fuck you can't find a bitch that ain't shady? I'm starting to think yo dick little. These bitches stay crossing you my nigga."

"First, don't ever reference my dick again, ole gay ass nigga. I don't know if his ass was lying or not, that's what I need to find out from that nigga in there. Selina said her home girl, cousin, or some muthafuckin body kickin' it with one of they asses and the niggas was fucked up the other night and running they mouth."

"You think we can trust her ass bruh?"

"Only time will tell. She's only heard about the bitch that crossed me, if she on that same shit, she'll meet her."

I started walking towards Kwame's crib, it was time to get to the bottom of some things. We needed some valid and valuable information and today was the day I was gonna get it. Muthafuckas was getting ready to feel me out here.

NAUTICA

*E*ver since baby girl been gone shit ain't been right. I can't tell you the last time my ass ate and of course me and Majik been at each other's throats day in and day out. We can't go a day without arguing about some stupid shit.

Majesti has been gone for over three weeks and I will be glad when she's found. I almost fainted when I got to school, and they told me she'd already been checked out. Well that was after I almost beat the shit outta the bitch in the front office. She knew got damn well she ain't never seen nobody but me and Majik picking up and dropping her off.

CoCo better hope her stupid ass don't ever have to face me. She don't know what kinda danger she's put baby girl in and if one hair on her head is touched, she don't have to worry about Majik fucking her up.

Majik went to the house he'd bought for her and she'd taken

all her clothes and whatever Majesti had over there. It looked like a nigga had been there and they all left in a hurry. That only means that her dumb ass let Draego talk her into some stupid shit.

I heard Majik come in slamming doors and shit. Walking down the stairs I went to see if we could somehow have peaceful day without any arguing.

"Hey babe, what's up? What you been doing all day?"

"What the hell you think I been doing? Looking for my got damn daughter!"

"Ok Majik, do it really take all that? All you had to do was answer the fucking question." So much for not arguing.

"What the fuck you mean do it take all that?"

"You can't just answer the question without all the extra shit!"

"You ain't gonna tell me how to fucking talk. It's your muthafuckin fault I'm in this shit, your fucking fault my daughter is missing!"

"Wait excuse me, what did you say? I know muthafuckin well you didn't just say what the fuck I think you said."

"You brought that bitch ass nigga into our lives. That muthafucka wouldn't be here if it wasn't for you. Now Majesti been kidnapped and Ahnais can't stop having nightmares. That's on you shawty!"

The shit that he just spit out his mouth was foul as fuck. Ain't no coming back from that. For him to sit there and blame me for something I had no control over was messed up on so many levels. Draego for one raped Ahnais before I even knew his sick twisted ass. I didn't make his baby mama a hoe, she chose to jump on the first dick that smiled in her face.

I left him standing right there in the middle of the living room and I headed upstairs to the room and began packing my shit. I damn sure wasn't bout to stay here and let him blame me for this bullshit. It took me about an hour and a half to pack all my shit, I don't know when I'd acquired all this shit I was lugging around. I smelled Majik smoking on some good trees while I drug my bags down to my car. This shit was heavy as hell, but I be damn if I asked his ass for help. He'd migrated to his man cave and probably didn't know I was leaving, he'll find out soon enough.

It took me four got damn trips to load up all my shit in my car and once I was done I jumped in and sped off. I still had the keys to the place I was sharing with Amaris, so that's where I was headed. I sent her a text letting her know I was going to be staying over there for a while. I was going to start back looking for my own place this week, I should've done that in the first place. I start school to finish my degree in two months, so by then I hope to have everything in order.

My phone started blowing up not even ten minutes after I sent Maris that text. I was getting calls from everyone back to back, I just didn't have the energy to answer any questions.

Auntie: you better be dead or in a coma you ugly lil bitch. That better be the only reason your funky ass ignoring my calls.

Auntie: and btw if yo ass ain't dead I'mma pop you upside yo head and cuss yo ass out.

I was just gonna have to take the consequences cause I didn't want to talk. I knew there wasn't nothing to eat at the house, so I stopped at the store to grab a few items. By the time I'd done a little shopping, taken everything out of my car, and straighten up the house, I was a tad bit exhausted. The situation that happened with Majik was weighing heavy on my mind. I replayed the words he said over and over in my mind and I eventually started believing it.

Luck was on my side today because not only was the lights still on here but so was the cable. I have no idea why, but won't he do it? There was no way I could survive without watching my reality shows and not to mention Power was due to start back up soon. Lord knows I love me some Ghost.

After cleaning the tub out, I ran me some steaming, nice hot bath water. I added some bubbles and one of those colorful Victoria Secret bath bombs. I've never used them before, but I heard it makes your skin feel silky smooth. I lit a bunch of candles I'd gotten from the store and popped open a bottle of wine.

Turning on some music, I was already on my second glass I'd only been in there just a little while. I don't know what snapped in me, but I all of a sudden got depressed. I started thinking about all the shit I've been through and I was over it. With nonstop tears running down my face, I felt defeated. All the beatings I received from the hands of Draego, the words Majik said to me, the look on Ahnais' face when she saw his face, and hearing the laughs of Majesti, all those flashbacks where popping up in my mind like lightning.

I grabbed my phone and drunkenly called Ahnais. I needed to tell her I was sorry. There was no need in me going on with this fucked up life, but I first needed to tell her I was sorry.

As soon as she answered the phone, I went straight in with my rant.

"I'm sorry cousin, I'm sorry he did that to you. It's my fault you saw him again and I'm sorry. I love y'all, please remember I loved y'all," I slurred

The last thing I heard was her calling my name over and over again, I saw blackness before I knew it.

NAUTICA

Sometime later...

I tried opening my eyes, but the light and this headache was making it super hard. I was in excruciating pain and I had no idea why. I groaned as I tried to sit up, but even sitting up at this point was too much.

"Ahhhhh!" I yelled out in a hoarse tone.

"Serves your stupid, dumb ass right!" I heard my auntie Frankie yell out.

Wait the hell is my auntie doing here and why is her crazy ass mad for now?

"Mama be nice."

"Auntie why are you yelling and why is my head pounding so damn hard?" I needed answers and I needed them like now.

"Your head need to hurt you bald headed, possum face, raccoon looking ass retard. Fuck was you thinking not answering the got damn phone when I call and drinking all that shit while in the tub? Drinking all that shit period?"

"First, Auntie how can I look like a possum and a raccoon? Second, I really don't know what you're talking about."

She jumped on the bed so damn quick nobody had a chance to stop it. She popped me upside my head and all I saw was stars. If she was a bitch on the street, we would have to shoot a quick fade. My fucking head was already hurting, and she just made it worse.

"Ask another stupid ass question like that again. Your fucking ass almost killed yourself and you asking stupid shit."

"Nautica what's wrong cousin? Why would you want to end your life, why would you do that to yourself, to us?" Amaris had tears in her eyes. I didn't know if it was her hormones or not.

All of a sudden, the events of last night played in my mind. The phone call and everything I'd been thinking.

"Everything is so messed up and it's all my fault."

"What are you talking about child?" My auntie asked walking back over towards me. I flinched cause you can't be too sure with her. "Girl ain't nobody about to touch you."

Ahnais helped me sit up and put a cool towel on my forehead after giving me an aspirin.

"Now get to talking Nautica. This ain't like you and you weren't raised to be a weak bitch. Lately you've been giving off weak bitch vibes and it's pissing me off."

Once she turned her back to me, so she could sit down, I

mocked her and stuck my tongue out. I felt for real like a five-year-old kid.

"Nautica keep acting like a kid and I'mma beat your ass like one."

How in the hell did she see? Her ass must got them super parent powers or something.

I sighed before going over everything from beginning to the end with them, starting with the things Majik had said to me. Again, the tears had began to flow and I wished like hell I could get myself together. I was so tired of feeling sorry for myself all the time and always crying. My auntie was right, this weak shit wasn't me.

"Nauti, fuck what Majik said, you know damn well this isn't your fault and me being raped had nothing to do with you. You didn't even know that animal at the time it happened."

"I know but like you and Majik both said, I brought him to you guys."

"Ooohhhh girl shut up. You making the back of my neck itch, stop all that whining. He said this, but I did this, oh shut the fuck up. You ain't responsible for how other muthafuckas move, you're only responsible for yourself. Now do some stupid shit like this again and you won't have to worry about dying cause I'mma end ya shit. Get up and clean yaself up and brush for funky ass teeth." She was walking around the room slamming shit. "Doing all that boo-hooing and yo' breath smelling like the ass of two homeless men. Where Majik limp noodle dick ass at anyway?"

She just got done clowning on my breath but gone ask me a

question. What kinda backwards ass shit was that? This lady is nuts. I sat my funky breath ass right on that bed like I ain't heard nothing. I let her continue on her rant about Majik and I slowly stood up to make my way to the bathroom. I felt worse standing up than I did sitting down. I was praying that after I got a good shower it made me feel a little better.

I could feel them looking at my every move, but they didn't have to worry about me doing anything crazy like this again. Hell, the way I was feeling at this point, I didn't want to even have another damn drink no time soon.

I brushed my teeth, flossed, and gargled with my mouthwash before jumping in the shower. While washing my body I had a thought, I'm done taking bullshit from men. I'm taking my power back. They wanted the strong Nautica, well dammit they're about to get it. From now on, all I was worrying about was getting my life in order. I wasn't gonna depend on no one else for my happiness. What pisses me off though is for Majik's stupid ass to blame me, but he is the one that came after me. I shot him down several times and he kept trying. It's all good though cause the new Nautica is about to blow their minds.

AHNAIS

I was so damn scared when I got that call from Nautica a few weeks ago. I don't know what I'd do if something was to happen to my cousin. We'd just gotten her back here with us. Majik had shit fucked up and after I spent forty-five minutes cussing him out, I ain't spoke to him since. I was up getting ready to take Yanni to camp. So, I was out, but she still needed something to do instead of sitting in the house looking stupid all day.

"Come on Yanni, hurry up before you're late!"

"Maaaaaa, why I gotta go to this camp?"

"Cause I said so, now get ya ass up, so we can go!"

"Okayyy, but you wouldn't want me to be snatched up like Majesti, now would you?"

"If they snatched you, they'd bring your ass right back. I'm sure of it."

"Now that's just rude! You gone miss me when I'm gone."

Why must this child aggravate me and this early in the damn morning. I needed to be out this door in the next twenty minutes in order to make it to work on time. Shit was already strange having people following me and staying at my damn job all day, as well as embarrassing. I had to come up with a bullshit as story as to why I had security. I know damn well them folks didn't believe me though.

Draiven was coming in when we were on our way out and he looked like pure shit. I'd barely seen him in the last few days and that wasn't gonna fly with me. I don't give a shit what they had going in the streets, home comes first.

"Nigga you done lost your mind. Fuck you thinking about bringing your lil dick ass in here like you didn't stay out all night?"

"Shawty I'm tired as fuck, so if you ain't about to use your mouth to suck this dick, I'mma need you to shut the fuck up. Take yo ugly ass to work man, I'm bout to go to bed." He looked at me and grabbed his dick. "I mean unless you bout to put yo mouth to work!"

"Nigga you got me fu-"

"Hey daddy, ummm where you were last night? I came in to talk to you and I waited up." Yanni came in interrupting me, but we both was waiting on an answer.

"I was working baby girl, get your stuff so you won't be late to camp. We'll chop it up when you get home today." She ran back upstairs to get whatever it was she left. "That nigga Majik fucking up man, me and Draiven having to pick up his slack.

With Majesti still missing and the shit going on with Nautica, he done turned into a got damn alcoholic."

"Fuck Majik, he wrong as hell for what he said to my cousin," I said grabbing my pharmacy lab coat, along with my keys, purse, and phone.

"Stay out they shit." He kissed me and made his way up the stairs, passing by mama on the way.

"Mama I don't get off until after seven, so can you please pick up Yanni at three? I'm pretty sure Draiven won't be able to."

"I'll pick up my own damn daughter. Don't be out here acting like I'mma for real deadbeat!" the nosey muthafucka yelled from upstairs.

I didn't even give his ass a response. I kissed my mama and walked out. I'm not gonna apologize for asking my mama to get my baby. The way he been moving lately I don't know what he on. One thing for certain though, we definitely gonna have to talk tonight. I understand he having to pick up Majik's slack, but he needs to remember that he does have a family and responsibilities.

I'd been busy from the moment I stepped into work. I've been on the go nonstop and was in desperate need of a break, but I'm almost certain I wasn't gonna get one no time soon though. I was in the middle of verifying this prescription when Selina walked up.

"Boss lady, you have a consultation," she said sounding all sad and shit. She been acting like she done lost her best fucking friend.

I know her and Lenyx been going through some stuff, but this girl was acting like she was on some suicide shit.

"Okay give me just one second." I didn't even bother looking up.

Walking over to the consultation counter, I went to assist the patient, so I could get back to my work. Sometimes these folks be asking the stupidest damn questions.

"Hi, wha- um, what can I help you with today?" when I finally looked up I saw a familiar face. I don't know who this man is, but it seems like everywhere I go, he's there. I need to let Draiven know about this shit. I looked around to see if my security detail was in the store and noticed them in the SUV.

"We just keep running into each other, it must be fate."

"How can I assist you today Sir?' I tried to keep it as professional as I could.

"It's something sexy about a professional woman. What do you suggest I use for severe allergies? I think it may be the pollen or something."

Looking at him, I couldn't see that there was anything wrong, but that didn't mean anything. Looks can be very deceiving and that's beside the point. Regardless of the situation, I still had to answer all questions.

"For something over the counter, I would suggest Claritin or Zyrtec."

"And where would that be, would you mind showing me?"

"If you know which one you want, I can have my Pharmacy Tech Selina here get it for you and ring you up."

"I'd be happier if you would do it."

"I apologize Sir, that's what they're here for. I have a lot of work I need to get back to, so if there isn't anything else, I can make sure you're taken care of."

"I guess if you're sure you can't assist me."

"You have a wonderful day Sir."

I didn't entertain him any further. There wasn't no point in it, the longer I went back and forth, the longer he'd try to engage me into a conversation.

This guy kept looking at me on some suspicious type shit and it was creeping me out. As I continued filling prescriptions, I discreetly pulled out my phone to send Draiven a quick text message. I needed them to see this man, my gut was tingling and when my gut tingles then something usually ain't right.

I went back to doing my job and put everything else that wasn't dealing with work on the back burner. I thought you were supposed to go to work to get away from your problems.

After Mr. Creeper left, my shift went by pretty quickly and since Draiven picked up Yanni, I was free to go straight home for once.

Walking to my car, I was busy texting the girls in a group text when I looked up and saw somebody standing near my driver side door with flowers in hand. I smiled before I had a chance to stop it.

"Why are you at my job and standing at my car? You know if my fiancé catches you here he'd kill you right?"

"Well that's a chance I'm willing to take. I mean look at you, who wouldn't?"

"So, what are you doing here?"

"I was wondering if I could take you out tonight. A beautiful woman like you should be treated like queen."

"I'm always treated like a queen, but since you're here, I guess you can take me out. But just this once, my fiancé is a psycho."

"Well since I only get one night with you, how bout you let me eat that pussy and give you some of this dick?"

I blushed, and I had no idea why those words made me feel butterflies.

"Where's my baby at Draiven?"

"At home with yo mama. Now answer my question, you gonna let me eat that pussy?"

"I meaannn I ain't gone stop you ya know!"

We carried our flirting inside my car and he drove us to wherever we were going. I asked several times to go home and change clothes, but he kept telling me that I was fine.

He ended up pulling up to this little quaint and quiet restaurant not far from my job. I'd never seen this place before.

"So, what's going on Draiven, why are you doing all of this?" I asked him once we were seated.

"What, I can't do something nice for my wife now?"

"I mean yeah, but lately you've forgotten you had a wife. Hell, a daughter too!"

"Don't do that! I will never forget family. I know shit been crazy shawty, so I felt the need to do a lil something for you."

"Well aren't you so sweet?"

I wondered where his car was and how he'd gotten to my job, but I didn't bother asking. We were having such a good time, laughing and joking about everything. We hadn't let loose like this in a long time. It was almost impossible to do, with both of us working and dealing with Yanni.

I was having so much fun on this date, I was dreading going home. An idea popped in my head but, before I asked Draiven, I sent my mama a text asking if she could keep Yanni until in the morning.

Once I got confirmation that everything was cool with my child, we finished up our food and hubby paid the check, so we could get up out of there. While waiting on Draiven to finish up, I was on my phone getting us a room. I didn't tell him what I was up to. When we got to the car, I just grabbed the keys out his hands and drove to our next destination. I don't know if he had something else planned for us, but oh well.

He was asking all kinds of questions up until I pulled into the Ritz-Carlton parking lot and it clicked what I was on. His crazy ass smirked and shook his head.

I was able to stop at Walmart to get me some things to handle my hygiene and as soon as we were checked into the room, I immediately jumped in the shower. Tryna fuck yo nigga with a musty, sweaty work pussy ain't the move.

Draiven was sitting on the edge of the bed when I got out the shower rolling up and I went and stood right in front of his ass butt naked. I'm glad I always kept some good smelling lotion up in my purse, cause I couldn't shower without using it afterwards.

Before I could make a move on him, this nigga picked me up, sat me in the chair while draping my legs over the arms of the seat. He squatted down in front of me and inserted two fingers inside of my pussy while gently sucking on my clit. The shit felt so good and he hasn't even really started doing anything yet. Taking his fingers out, he spread my lips open and dove in face first. Sucking and licking all of my juices, this nigga was eating my pussy like he'd gotten caught doing something and was trying to apologize for it.

He used his tongue and licked from my pussy on down to my asshole, flicking it fast as hell. I promise it felt like he was snatching out my soul.

"Yessssssssaahhhh baby. Ohhhhh fuckkk! I yelled out while I rubbed the top of his head.

This went on for over thirty minutes and I was loving every minute of it. Laying on the bed, he continued his assault with his mouth and I was losing all common sense. I couldn't let him have the upper hand like this, so I quickly moved his head back, jumped up, and pushed him on his back. I climbed on his face and put all this pussy is his mouth. I was on the verge of cumming and I knew it was gonna be a strong one.

"Oooohhhhh shiiaaatttttttt, muthafucka got damn." I was shaking like I was a crackhead needing a fix.

I fully understood now how these niggas felt when they got out that one good nut that had em' feeling so good, it made em' throw up gang signs. I was ready to jump up and holla, "Crrrriii-ipppp. Caaaaaaarrrrrippppppp!"

Still in a daze, I didn't notice when he climbed on top of me, but I quickly snapped out it when he put that big ass dick off his in me.

"Got damn girl! This shit good and fuckin wet."

I was put in so many positions and I was loving every moment of it. I was surprised by Draiven's actions tonight, but I sincerely appreciated it. I was concerned about where our relationship was headed. This showed me that he was still invested in this relationship and I love this fuck nigga.

Majik

I've been fucking up since my baby been gone. CoCo told me she was gonna get me back, but in the words of that nigga Jay Z, she didn't have to get a nigga back like that. She knows I don't play about my seed, so she didn't do shit but manage to piss me off more and push up her death date. Her wack ass family about to add another picture to their missing person flyer.

CoCo know what I'm capable of, but her dick brain ass done let some pussy ass muthafucka talk her into doing something she can't take back.

On top of my daughter missing, I done managed to lose my got damn girl. I don't know what possessed me to say that stupid ass shit to Nautica. I'd been drinking all day and it just came out. They say a drunk mind tells no lies, but in this case that shit ain't true.

I'd been tryna call Nautica, but she declines every call. She reads my text and don't respond. I let her have her cool down time, but now she bout to piss me off. She knows I love her ass man. I'mma just have to pull up on her ass I guess.

I had to put my plans for pulling up on Nauti to the side for now. I heard through a few people that CoCo been keeping in touch with her ugly ass friend Kaycie. That stupid hoe running around here talking too damn much. It's a good thing for me, but bad for her.

Knock Knock Knock

Who in the fuck is this at my door?

I looked at my camera monitors and saw Lenyx, Draiven, my pops, and my uncle. I wondered what the fuck these niggas was doing at my house.

I opened the door looking at them a little suspect. These muthafuckas ain't never popped up at my shit together.

"You gonna let us in bitch?" Lenyx pushed me out the way.

"Fuck y'all want?"

My dad stopped in his tracks and turned to glare at me. That big amazon ass muthafucka think he scare somebody.

"Majik watch your mouth, don't be disrespectful!" He gave me another look and I couldn't help but to laugh.

"Old man who you think you scaring? I'll fold yo old ass up. Fuck around and karate chop you in yo bad back."

"Don't let the gray hair fool you nigga. I'll beat yo ass like I shoulda when you was a baby."

We cut up for a minute making our way to the living room. Me and my pops was close as hell. I really looked up to his ass.

"But for real though, what y'all fellas doing over this way?"

"Came to check up on your suicidal ass. All you do is sit your big chested ass in this house and drink that rock gut ass liquor and feel sorry for yourself. My niece needs to be found and we still got work to do out here." This muthafucka Lenyx was about to piss me off.

"So, what's this supposed to be, some kind of intervention? Y'all gone read me letters y'all wrote for me and shit?"

"This ain't no laughing matter muthafucka!" Now here Draiven go with his bullshit.

"Man, if that's what y'all came for I'm good, so you can politely get the hell out my shit. Y'all actually holding me up from going to check on some shit."

"So, we keeping secrets now?" Lenyx spoke up again.

Got damn these niggas too got damn sensitive for me. They cry more than Majesti and Yanni put together. I'm glad I know these fools are some for real goons cause the way they're acting right now, one wouldn't know.

"Tinker bell calm the fuck down. Wasn't nobody keeping nothing from yo ass. I heard CoCo's ugly ass friend Kaycie may know where she at. They say the hoe been out running her muthafucka mouth."

"So, what's up, what's the move?"

"I was bout to go check it out until y'all Power Ranger asses came walking up in here holding me up."

"Well shit nephew let's go!" my uncle old ass said getting up. These two AARP niggas need something to entertain they ass.

I don't know why they think they can still run with us. The hell they gonna do if we get in a shoot-out? They'll been done threw their hip out.

"Hell, you think you is Unc, muthafuckin John Wayne? Let

me guess that's Clint Eastwood?" I asked him while pointing at my pops.

"Bring yo ass on, let's see what this young lady gotta say about my grand baby!"

I looked back and forth between the two of them a few times to see if these niggas was for real. I got my answer when they stood up ready to go. I had to glance back at the fellas to see what they thought about this shit. Lenyx shrugged his shoulders and Draiven stood up and made his way to the door.

I couldn't do shit but shake my head and follow behind them as I locked up my house. I wasn't tryna spend my day with these geriatric patients, but I wasn't gonna be stupid enough to tell them that. I'd hate to have to break my old man's hip.

We didn't wanna be caught at ole girl's crib in broad daylight, so we made a few stops until it was time to head over there. As soon as the clock hit eleven p.m. it was time to head out. I was glad as hell cause being with they asses all day done gave me a damn headache. My fucking mama done call my phone all day fussing cause my pops was still out tryna kick it. That shit ain't on me, she better talk to her husband about all that.

It didn't take us long at all to get to that slut bucket ass bitch's house. Her ass wasn't at home when we got here, so we decided to sit in her shit and wait on her.

These fool ass niggas was eating snacks, watching ESPN, and talking shit back and forth with they feet keep kicked up on the damn table.

About fifteen minutes later the doors were being unlocked

and I had to shush these niggas up. They couldn't act right for shit. Her stupid ass was too busy gossiping on the phone, she didn't even realize people were in her house.

"Oooh shit!" she yelled out while holding her chest and dropping her phone.

I could hear the person on the other end calling her name while she stared at me like a dear caught in headlights. I put my finger up to my lips telling her to be quiet as I quickly grabbed her phone to see who was on the other end. I was hoping it was CoCo, but I wasn't that lucky. I hung up on the call, so I could hurry up and deal with this ugly mutt. I always wondered why cute girls hung around ugly ass friends.

"What up lil ugly ass girl that think she the shit?"

"Umm hey Majik. Why are you here in my house?"

"Bitch, this ain't no open-ended questioning session. We ask the questions and yo dirt face ass answer them. That's how this about to work," Lenyx spoke up.

She started fidgeting and looking around before we even asked her the first question. That let me know off rip she had something to hide. I can't trust a bitch that can't look me in the eye.

"Fuck you acting all nervous for, you been basing?" Draiven asked and we all busted out laughing. This fool over here sounding like Tupac in Poetic Justice.

I didn't have time to clown around with these fools all night. It was time to get down to business.

"Kaycie come on over here and have a seat. I need to ask you a few questions." She hesitantly sat on her couch, looking scared as hell. "You heard from CoCo?"

She quickly shook her head no, so I could tell what time of situation this was gonna be. I pulled out my gun go show her I wasn't playing. Before I could even ask her my next question my pops sat down on the raggedy ass coffee table in from of her and started talking.

"Listen young lady, I'm an old man and I'm usually not out in these streets this time of night. Now I'm out trying to find my granddaughter, and something tells me you can assist me with that. Now you can do this the hard way, or we can do it the easy way, that's all up to you. I can guarantee you'll die in here tonight though if you keep playing stupid. Now we gonna try this again, be careful and think before you answer."

I was gonna let my pops have that Lean on Me, Morgan Freeman speech. I wasn't bout to be nice to her ass. She could either answer the question or get popped in her dome, choice was hers.

"Kaycie have you heard from CoCo? Remember think smart before you answer?" I reminded her cocking my pistol back.

"Well umm I... yeah she umm." She was stumbling over her words, irritating my ass.

"I, I, I... bitch if your Porky the Pig sounding ass don't hurry up and answer the question, I swear I'mma shoot you." Draiven pointed his pistol towards her head. That nigga was getting pissed and I don't blame him.

"Okay wait no. She calls me when she can."

"Where she at and what she say?"

"She didn't exactly tell me where she was at, but she did say she wasn't far and when you were handled she could come back."

"Is that right?" I stared at her for a few seconds. "Aight so check this out get ya shit, you coming with me."

CoCo wanna play with me, it's time I show Atlanta why not to fuck with something of mine. Next up, these got damn Italian muthafuckas. Them son of a bitches getting on nerves and making my ass itch.

AMARIS

I don't know if my hormones were on ten or if this nigga playing me for stupid. Ever since I told him about this pregnancy his ass been moving funny. I'mma have to continue watching him closely. One thing for sure, I'll kill his ass dead if he thinks he gonna have me being a baby mama. Yeah, I think the fuck not.

It was time to go meet Ahnais for lunch and of course I was running late. This baby had me so drained, half the time I didn't even want to get up out of bed. I wasn't looking forward to this conversation we needed to have anyway. I'd finally reached out to Solomon and I had a meeting set up to have lunch with him in a few days. She may not be interested in hearing what he gotta say, but I was.

I pulled up to IHOP and almost tripped over my feet I was moving so fast. That omelet and pancakes was calling my name.

She sent me a text saying she was pulling up, so I waited up front a few minutes.

"Sissstterrr!" I yelled out hugging her.

"Sup stranger? Bitches get in house dick and forget about the little people that was there with them in the drought."

"Girl bye! You act like I don't talk to your needy ass every day. If you ain't calling me, ya mammy, or Nautica's ass calling. Y'all act like I ain't never been a parent before."

"Bitch you ain't." She laughed while we were being seated.

"You forgot it takes a village to raise your grown ass daughter."

Just as I mentioned Yanni, she was Face Timing me. This little girl must have known I was talking about her.

"Hey A'yanni."

"TeTe, you coming to get me today?"

"I hadn't planned on it, but I will. Why didn't you just come with your mama, now I gotta come all the way back that way."

"I asked her, but you know how dramatic she is. I wasn't here for it today."

I don't know where this girl gets half of the shit she says from.

"Yanni don't get your ass beat playing with me!"

I could see Yanni rolling her eyes and I could only laugh. After confirming with her that I'd pick her up later on today, I hung up to finish my lunch date Ahnais.

It was as if this conversation wasn't meant to happen cause just as I was starting it up, I got another phone call. Looking at it, I noticed it was Nautica.

"What's up bihh?" she asked when I answered.

"Shit, out eating with Ahnais."

"Oh, you bitches ain't think about me huh? Fuck y'all hoes then!"

"Girl stop being all sensitive, we just grabbing a bite to eat. Bring your ugly ass by here if you're out and about. We haven't ordered yet."

"Good cause I was gonna crash any damn way. Send me y'all location, I'll be there in a little bit."

It was a good thing she was already out cause her ass would've been missing out, I'm hungry as hell.

I hope I could finish this conversation with my sister before Nautica got here. I didn't want things to be all serious and whatnot while we were eating and enjoying each other's company.

"Nautica on the way so we might as well wait to order our food. It won't take her long to get here."

"That's cool, I already know what I'mma eat anyway."

"Before she gets here I need to talk to you about something. So, you know that guy Solomon who supposed to be our father?" She rolled her eyes and smacked her lips before I could even get out what I wanted to say. "Don't be like that Ahnais, I wanna meet up with him and hear what he gotta say."

"For what Maris? He ain't never been in our lives or did shit for us. Why would you want to even associate with that man? That shit is stupid!"

"It's not stupid, it's something that I need to do for myself. If you can't understand that I'm sorry but I need to do it."

"Whatever that's on you, but don't expect me to have a kumbaya moment with y'all. I don't want shit to do with his deadbeat ass."

"Well whatever Ahnais, that's on you."

"You know his people after Draiven and the guys, what you think is gonna happen if he meets up with you?"

I thought about all that and it didn't deter me wanting to still meet him. I guess I'll have to cross that bridge when I get there. When he first came back I had no intentions on meeting him, didn't even want to think about it. I don't know what made me want to change my mind, all I know is I want to do it.

About fifteen minutes later Nautica came sashaying in like she was on a runway. Ahnais was sitting mad not saying shit, which I knew she would do. That's exactly why I wanted to get the conversation out the way.

"Hello darlings," she spoke sounding like a rich white woman and air kissing us.

"Bitch you do know you're broke as shit right? Why in the hell are you talking like you crazy?" I laughed at no her crazy ass while flagging down the waitress. I didn't have time for her shenanigans today.

"Don't hate bitches! I'm just practicing for when I become rich."

We ordered our food quickly and sent our waitress on her way. Her ass was way too happy for my liking. I didn't trust people that was always smiling.

"You and Majik made up yet?" I couldn't help but to laugh at the look on her face.

"Who is Majik?" This girl really asked me that with a straight face. I cannot deal with her craziness at the moment.

"Girl I'm not about to play with you."

"He been calling and messaging me, I don't have shit to say to him though. I'm good on him, but can you tell me why Ahnais sitting over there looking like she about to explode?"

"She calls herself mad at me. I told her I wanted to meet up with Solomon and she butt hurt."

"First ya'll hoes can stop talking about me like I'm not fucking here. Second, it's stupid as hell for you to wanna meet a person that ain't never gave a shit about you, but hey you do you boo."

"Whatever, it ain't even about that. I have questions I need answers for and he wi-" I stopped talking in the middle of my sentence when I thought I saw a face I know I've seen before.

Nautica started looking around trying to figure out what it was I was looking at.

"You look like you bout to pop off. What's wrong with you bihh?"

"Ya'll remember the bitch I told ya'll about from the grocery store that day?" Once they thought back to what I was referring to they both shook their head. "That's the bitch over there at that table staring at me like she wanna eat my pussy."

They looked around until they saw who I was referring to. That Toadfish looking ass hoe was still looking at me staring with a smirk on her face. If I wasn't so hungry and pregnant, shawty would have to throw them hands. This baby got me eating everything in sight, every hour. It pissed me off even more that she was sitting this close to me.

"Can I help you with something? Fuck is you staring at my cousin like you in fucking love or some shit?"

"Girl bye, I ain't worried about nobody over there. Oh, and nah I ain't in love, but her nigga in love wit this pussy."

"It's always that one bap ass hoe that gotta be seen," Ahnais spoke up.

The waitress was walking past, and I quickly stopped her.

"Excuse me ma'am, how long before my food come out? I need to be fully fed and full before I go to jail for beating this hoe ass."

She looked at me not knowing how to answer my question but gave me a half laugh while still looking stupid.

"Ummmm, your food will be out in just a few ma'am. Is there anything else I can get for you?"

"Nope, I'm good!" I told her giving her attitude and I really didn't even mean to.

Looking at this unknown bitch with this fucked up smirk on her face was putting me in a place I didn't like. I know for a fact that Jaysun out here playing me for a fool, this bitch ain't throwing major shade for nothing. My leg was bouncing up and down so fast and hard, I thought it was gonna break. Nautica put her hand over my knee to try and stop it, I guess she noticed it since she was sitting right next to me.

I took a few more pics of this broad to add to my collection. Every time I see her, I was gonna snap a photo. I wanted proof of every time this chic was in my presence. I haven't confronted Jaysun about this woman yet, but tonight was gonna be the night.

It was time I get everything in my life sorted out. I don't know if it's the fact that I am having a baby, but I want everything in order.

When our food finally came out, we ate and enjoyed our time together without paying that lil bitch any more attention. She did everything she could do to try and get my attention. I wasn't with the shit, so I ignored her. If there ever came a time that I needed to handle her, I will. Until then, that mud duck ass hoe was invisible to me at the moment.

I made it home a little after bit after nine and I already knew Jaysun would be home waiting. I purposely went all day without answering any of his calls. He knew nothing had happened to me for the simple fact we had them got damn details everywhere we went. If I didn't answer his calls though, he tended to act like a damn bratty ass child.

As soon as I walked into the living room where he was sitting and waiting, he walked up on me and grabbed my purse without saying a word. The first thing he did was grab my phone. After a few seconds of him having the phone in his hand, I heard his ringing.

"Ohh okay, so I see your shit do work. So, can you tell me why I ain't from you? I done called and texted your ass several times today."

"You need to be worried about your bitches out in the streets instead of clocking my fucking moves nigga."

"Amaris what the fuck is you talking about? I swear this baby got you on some bullshit!"

"Nah muthafucka, my baby ain't got shit to do with nothing. You just ended up getting me pregnant before I realized you was a fuck nigga!"

"You better watch yo fucking mouth, for real shawty. Now either you can let me know what your issue is or get the fuck on and shut the hell up."

"If I remember correctly, you walked up in my space. I didn't bother you, it was the other way around."

"Man stop it with all the childishness. What the fuck is your issue?"

"I don't have an issue; however, I would appreciate it if you told your bitches to stop approaching me. You need to get them hoes in line and make them stay in their fucking lane."

"Stop with all the talking in code and shit. I ain't got no fucking bitches to get in line, so I don't know what your ass even talking about."

I unlocked my phone and went to my photo gallery. I pulled up the picture I had taken earlier and put the phone in his face as close as I could.

"So, you don't know who this person is?" I asked holding the phone close to his nose.

He pushed my hand back some and snatched the phone out of my hand. He looked at it closely and frowned up his face.

"Who the fuck is this supposed to be?"

"Okay keep playing stupid, but like I said, keep your bitches away from me. Don't let your dirt find its way home cause when it does I'mma be gone. That's a promise."

I didn't bother waiting for him to give a reply. I quickly walked off and took my ass upstairs. Walking inside of Destiny's room, I sat on her bed and held her pillow and cried. I don't know if I was crying from hurt, this baby and my hormones, or missing Destiny and feeling guilt. I was feeling guilty cause here I am about to have a baby and Jaysun not too long ago lost her. I know that he is not mentally ready to handle this, but at the same time I didn't get pregnant or purpose. Did we do anything to prevent it? No, but it still wasn't planned. I wished like hell I would have gotten more time to know her. I laid down just reminiscing on the times I was able to spend with her and before long I felt myself dozing off.

"Hey Amaris, wake up, come on silly wake up!"

I sat up and groggily, rubbing my eyes. I couldn't believe I was seeing who I was looking at.

"Did I die or something?" I asked scared

"No crazy, it's just a dream. I had to come and tell you it's okay, I want to be a big sister."

"Wait how did you know what I was thinking?"

"I'm in heaven, I know and see everything."

"We miss you so much Destiny!"

"You guys have to let me go, I know you love me. Tell my daddy it's okay, I'm happy for you guys. He has to move on or he'll never be happy."

"He hasn't been doing too good without you."

"Do me a favor Amaris."

"Anything for you baby girl."

"Promise me you will always take care of my daddy. Stay by his side and protect him. He won't last without you with him."

"I got you cupcake, I got you."

"Tell daddy I'm having a ball up here with my mommy. He doesn't have to be sad anymore."

"I'll tell him, I wish you could come back to us. It's been so hard since you've been gone." Tears rolled down my face as I trembled.

"I'm always around and watching. Tell Yanni don't be tryna replace me." She laughed trying to lighten the mood. "Take care of my baby brother and I'll be back to talk to you again soon."

She slowly began gliding backwards as she began to fade. I was doing everything in my power to keep her with me.

"Wait! Wait Des please don't leave yet, come back! Don't leave us again, please don't"

"Remember I'll always be with ya'll. You have to let me go! It's okay, tell my daddy it's okay!"

"WAITTTTTT DON'T GO!"

I jumped up out of my sleep with fresh tears streaming down my face. I looked around searching for Destiny and realized I was still in her bed. The dream I just had was something out of a movie. I have never experienced anything like that before in my life. I'm positive no one would believe me if I told them what had happened.

Destiny coming to me in my dreams made me realize one thing, no matter what happened I was going to be alright. I know she was watching over me and this baby and she was going to protect us.

I didn't bother getting up to go to my own bed, I snuggled up with the teddy bear she used to love holding onto and closed my eyes back with a huge smile on my face.

DRAIVEN

A nigga been working overtime tryna make sure my family is safe and this wedding goes off without any issues. Kwame checked shit out with Solomon and his camp and just like he said, that muthafucka had some snakes in his camp. I almost beat Kwame's ass cause he shoulda had all the information on them fools from the beginning. I'm still wondering why them niggas coming after us, but I guess it all boils down to greed.

I've had to deal with my girl bitching day in and day out about Amaris wanting to meet up with that nigga Solomon. I don't see why she give a fuck, but apparently, she does. As long as that clown ass muthafucka don't fuck with sis, hell I'm good with it.

I'd just gotten up to get my day started and of course I had to wash my balls before I did anything. With the life I led, I never knew when it would be my last day. I damn sure didn't wanna get caught with some stanking ass nuts. I didn't need the coroner talking about 'this nigga had all this money and couldn't even keep his balls smelling fresh'. Hell nah, after I jumped in the shower I picked out my outfit for the day which was some Versace basketball shorts, a Versace T-shirt and the perfect slides to match it.

I heard my phone ringing somewhere in the room and when I finally got to it, I saw I'd missed about six calls from the fellas. Just as I was about to call one of them back, the phone rang again. Looking at the screen I saw it was Majik.

"What up my nigga?"

"Hell, you been doing, playing in ya ass? We done called ya muthafuckin ass several times."

"Nigga you ain't my bitch, stop clocking my moves. Fuck you want?"

"Pack up ya shit cowgirl, we gotta go make that run, just got the call."

"Man, fuckkkkk right now?"

The last thing I expected for him to tell me was that we had to go holla at Marcelo. I didn't think we was gonna have to meet up with him again until it was finally time to take over.

"Yeah nigga, so hurry up. We on the way to scoop you up, we gotta make it to the strip. The plane gassed up and ready to go."

I hung up and tried to figure out how I was gonna break this to my family. I was supposed to do some shit with Yanni later and now that shit wasn't gonna happen. I already know she was gonna make me pay for this shit. While I was upstairs away from everybody, I went ahead and packed a quick bag and sat it by my room door.

There wasn't a point in me hiding, I needed to go ahead and get this conversation over with. I went looking for everyone and found them in the kitchen making a late breakfast. I hoped I was still here when Ahnais was done cooking. If she couldn't do anything else, she could cook. I think that's what reeled me in, her good pussy and her cooking.

"You finally decided to get your ass out the bed?" Ahnais said looking up from the stove.

"Daddy, I put my finger under your nose to make sure you were still breathing."

"Is that what I was smelling in my sleep? I thought I smelled butt, I thought I was dreaming."

"Uhhh DENIED! I'm always clean, tuhh, you tried it," she laughed as I kept poking my finger in her ear. "What we doing today old man?"

"DENIED! I'm far from old, tuhh you tried it," I said mocking her using her hand movements and facial expressions.

I was buying time and praying that this conversation went by as smooth as possible.

"I need to holla at y'all real quick."

"Aww hell this nigga done cheated," Mama Frankie shouted out.

"Old woman go adjust yo wig and fix yo dentures, ain't nobody cheating."

"What's going Draiven and don't talk about my mama."

"I gotta make a quick run across the border and I'mma be

gone for at least a few days. I know Yanni we were supposed to do something today baby girl, but I promise I'll make it up to you when I get back."

"Yanni go to your room for a minute, I need to talk to your daddy right quick."

"Oh lord, she about to be dramatic."

"I'mma dramatically beat your ass if you don't get the hell up to your room."

"That ugly ass heffa mouth is reckless, I don't know where she gets that shit from. Ya'll better get her ass under control," Frankie said, mad as hell.

Everybody stopped what they were doing, including Yanni and just stared at Frankie. I can't believe she really said that shit. Her mouth is the most reckless I've ever heard in my damn life.

"Really mama, really?

"What?"

I just shook my head. I didn't have time to get into an argument with my crazy ass mother in law right now. I know them fools will be here in a few and I needed to chop it up with my wife real quick.

"Why are you just now saying something Draiven? I'm sure you been knowing about this shit."

"You sound dumb as hell man, why the fuck would I promise my damn child I'd take her somewhere today if I knew I was leaving? I just got the call a lil while ago."

"What's going on then? Is everything okay?" She went from yelling to concerned with her bipolar ass. I think all them got that crazy gene.

"I don't know yet, I'll update you when I know more myself." Just as I said that the doorbell rang. I almost smiled cause I was saved by the bell. That question and answer session was not the move and I was tired of trying to answer some shit I didn't have the answers to.

I called Yanni back downstairs and had a lil talk with her before I went to make sure my security team was on their shit. The last thing I needed was something to happen to my damn family and I'm across the border.

After Lenyx and Majik was done aggravating my wife, about thirty minutes later we were out the door. I could tell my daughter was pissed at me, but it wasn't nothing I could do about it. She looks forward to our daddy and daughter dates that I plan once a week.

"So, what's up, why the hell Celo need to see us? I know his money ain't fucked up cause that ain't never been a problem."

"You know how he is man, he didn't give out any details," Majik said on his phone.

I'd be willing to bet he was on the phone begging Nautica to take his stupid ass back. I haven't known her all my life or no shit like that, but I know her well enough to know that she is stubborn as hell. It was gonna take a wing and a prayer for him to earn her heart back.

"Aye we taking Jaysun on this trip with us. I already cleared it with Celo." He looked up again and right back down. "Since he bout to link up with us on this shit, he needed to get with us on this meeting.

"I'm cool with it, but do you think all of us should be gone like this at the same time? Shit don't feel right to me bruh."

"Same shit I was thinking about dawg," Lenyx chimed in.

"We pay our team good money for shit like this. They know if anything happens to anyone of them, their ass gonna be dead as fuck."

We made it to Jaysun crib to scoop him and chopped it up with sis before we left. Nobody felt comfortable leaving her by herself, so we argued until she agreed to go stay at my house until we got back. She didn't like it, but I didn't give a fuck, as long as she was safe.

Once everybody was situated we was on our way. I couldn't imagine why we needed to take this meeting on such a short notice, but I guess I'll find out soon enough.

The meeting...

We made it to Mexico and was finally pulling up to Marcelo's estate.

"Gahh damn! Niggas living like this?" that nigga Jaysun was in awe, but we've seen this shit a million times. I had the same muthafuckin reaction though the first time I saw it.

When we made it to the steps the door opened, and Carmen appeared looking beautiful as always.

"Hola mis hijos," she spoke to us in her thick accent. She loved calling us her sons. Not only did she refer to us as her sons, she treated us like it every time she saw us.

"Hola ma Carmen."

"Hola Carmen," Lenyx spoke up.

"Hola ma," Majik said.

We all gave her a hug one by one as she led us inside. We knew our way around, but I think it made her feel good to show us some hospitality.

"Ma Carmen, this is Jaysun. He's new to the team," I told her introducing the homie.

"Si, hola mi hijo." She of course hugged and kissed him on the cheek. She always made us feel like part of the family, so I know she was gonna treat him the same.

"Hello, how are you?" he hugged her back just as Celo came strolling in slowly. Something looked off and different about him, but I couldn't put a finger on it.

"Don't get too comfortable with my wife hijo," Marcelo joked with him.

"Never that boss man," Jaysun laughed and shook Marcelo's hand. "I'm Jaysun, nice to finally meet you."

I could see Celo was accepting Jaysun's ass quick, that wasn't normal for him, so I knew he would fit in quick with the family.

"Let's go to my office fellas."

We made our way to his oversized office and he gave each one of us an expensive ass cigar.

"So, what's good Celo, hell we need to come down here for?"

"It's time fellas, I can't do this anymore. I'm sick and I want to spend the last of my days traveling with Carmen. She deserves it."

"Fuck you mean you sick?" I didn't like hearing this shit cause on the real, this man has been nothing but good to us.

"Is that why you getting out?" Majik asked looking hurt as well.

"Yo dawg what you mean you sick? Come on stop talking in codes and let us know the deal." Lenyx wanted to know.

I think each one of us was feeling this shit. We've been working with Celo for a long ass time and he was more than a connect, he was family.

"I have cancer, hijos."

"DAMN!" we all said at the same time.

"Whatever you need us to do, we got you Celo," I assured him.

"Yeah, we got you man," Majik co-signed, walking up to him patting him on the back.

"So, Roman Barassi is dead and left his son everything. Solomon isn't as coldblooded as his father. I have a meeting set up with him in a few days."

"Shit, I got word that he ain't the one after us. Some muthafuckas in his camp wanted us to think it was him to get rid of him. They figured they could get rid of us all, still waiting to find out a lil bit more information."

"You fellas are about to be ahead of a powerful organization. You can't afford to let things slip in the cracks, for your safety and your family's." He sat down out of breath and holding his chest. I ran over to his desk and poured him a glass of water from the bar. "I'm okay, I'm okay! I need ya'll to go into this with your eyes wide open. I'm not gonna bury ya'll, you're gonna bury me."

"Stop talking crazy old man, ain't nobody burying nobody. We on it," I informed him.

We stayed and talked with Marcelo for a little while longer before we called it a night. Tomorrow will come before you know it and we were gonna have to get up quite early to start our day. It was a lot of shit we had to learn from him in just a short few days, so we didn't have time to waste.

I went to my room I was staying in with a heavy heart and a lot of shit on my mind. Only thing that would make shit better was seeing my wife and daughter's face. That's exactly what I did, I called them and after that I took my ass to sleep.

LENYX

I'd been back home from our trip to Mexico for about a week now and a nigga been going full force ever since. We didn't want to take on the role of the new connect in Atlanta just yet, but shit at this moment we didn't have a choice. Marcelo has done a lot for us over the years and we couldn't in no way tell that man no. Our plan was to make sure we had the situation with the Barassi crew handled first, but that was impossible. We also wanted to make sure my niece Majesti was home and CoCo handled.

It's going on a month and a half and I miss that lil girl something serious, so I can only imagine what Majik is going through.

I got a few calls from Selina asking to meet up and I'd be lying if I said I didn't miss her ass. We had gotten pretty close in the small amount of time we'd spent together. I had a little bit of time today I could spare to meet up with her, so I was gonna take advantage of it. In a way, I wanted to see if she really was the opps or if I could trust her.

I'd sent her a text message to come by my house when she got off work today. Looking at the time on the clock, she was due to be over here within the next twenty to thirty minutes. I looked around the place to make sure shit was straight and nothing was out of order. I didn't have to worry about shit from another bitch being here cause I never brought a random ass hoe to where I laid my head. I smashed a few thot bitches since we been on hiatus, but I wasn't trusting them hoes like that.

The doorbell rung and looking at my phone her ass was right on time. As soon as I opened up the door and saw Selina, I was immediately taken aback. Shawty came here looking good as hell. Before I even spoke to her, I left her at the door and ran in the living room, grabbed the blanket off the back of the couch and took it back to the front door.

She was looking at me like I was crazy, but I had a reason for doing that shit. I didn't need her fine ass altering my decisions. I wrapped the blanket completely around her. I wish I could cover up her face as well, but I know that was going a little overboard.

"Ummm hey to you too Lenyx! What the hell are you doing?"

"That ain't important, just keep that around you like that while you're here shawty."

"Whatever Lenyx, I guess," she said walking into the living room in front of me.

I glanced at her ass and shook my head

Got damn shawty fine!!

"So, what's up? What we need to talk about?" I got straight to the point the moment she sat down on the couch.

"Why are you being so cruel and mean to me? What else do I have to do to prove to you I'm not out to get you?"

"Let me ask you this shawty. If the roles were reversed and I was somehow affiliated with the people you got beef with and coming after you, would you not side eye me?

"I mean I get where you coming from, but you're putting your issues you had with your past bitch on me and that's not fair to me." She had tears in her eyes and I was starting to feel bad.

I never wanted to be the type of person to insert past shit in my present. At the same time, I didn't know if she was being used like Tatiana was. That bitch lied about a lot of shit she said before we snuffed her ass.

"Man stop all that crying and shit. If you gonna be with a savage ass nigga, you gonna have to tighten up shawty."

She looked at me and rolled her eyes.

"I'm not a punk if that's what you're implying."

"We'll see about that ma. So, you say you all for me huh, what if it comes down to you having to choose between me and your cousin? What you gone do?"

She sat looking crazy and thinking about what I asked her. About two minutes later, she finally answered my question.

"I mean it ain't like I grew up with her or nothing like that. Yeah, she my cousin but it ain't like Nautica, Ahnais, and Amaris."

"So, if I killed the bitch, you gone still be able to look me in my face without any resentment?"

"It's like this of course nobody wants their family to die, but I know for a fact she'd sell me out in a minute. Shit, who's to say she ain't using me now? I ain't fucked with her since I heard them talking that night."

"Aight shawty we'll see."

I was willing to see where this shit would go between us, but I'd be lying if I said I trusted her ass fully. This situation put a bad taste in my mouth. Yeah, true enough I shouldn't take my trust issues I had with Tori out on her, but it is what it is.

I kicked it with shawty for a minute, just catching up. During the time she was here, I had to resist temptation to bend her thick ass over the couch.

Just as I was about to say fuck it and drop this dick off up in her ass, my phones began ringing off the damn hook.

"Aye bro you heard from Amaris?" Majik asked sounded like some shit was bout to pop off.

"Naw, what's going on?"

"Meet me at Draiven's crib asap!"

"One the way!" I hung up quickly putting my shoes on.

"Aye get ya shit and come on!"

"What's going on?"

"Selina don't ask no questions right now, just get your stuff and come on."

I was taking her with me cause the way that nigga sounded shit may be popping off and I didn't wanna have her in harm's way.

Here we go. It's always some shit going on!

NAUTICA

I was about to lose my mind worrying about Amaris. She'd been missing all day, and nobody has heard from her. After calling her phone over and over and not getting an answer, I broke down and called Ahnais and she'd been tryna call her too.

Somehow, she slipped away from her security detail and decided to go out on her own. We pulled up her location and when we got there, her car, phone, and purse was the only thing we found. Well the only thing we saw cause the guys shooed us away.

We all made it to Ahnais and Draiven's house and I was trying my best to hear what they were saying. I didn't wanna be around Majik, but at this point I didn't have a choice. I was gonna just have to bite my tongue and deal with it.

They called us in the living room and I didn't like the look on their faces. Something in the pit of my stomach was telling me that this was gonna end bad and they didn't have good news. I felt myself about to have an anxiety attack.

"You good Nauti?" Majik pulled to me the side and questioned.

"Don't call me that! Don't fucking call me that." I don't know what it was but hearing him call me what Majesti was known for calling me just really set me off. I missed her smart mouthed ass like crazy and I'd do anything if I could just see her one more time.

"Aye what the fuck is wrong with you man? You better chill yo ass the fuck out wit all that crazy shit."

"Don't call her crazy Majik. You think you were the only person suffering from shit that's been going on? Nah! But instead of you trying to comfort each other, you decided to say some bullshit and had her feeling some type of way. So please keep your crazy comments to yourself."

"I see this about to be cuss out Majik day!"

Everybody had made it to the house, including Jaysun and he looked like he was ready to murder the whole city of Atlanta.

"So, we know CoCo and that bitch ass nigga ran off with my niece, seems like he done teamed up with them bitch ass Italians. They got Amaris," Draiven told us. I knew it was something he didn't wanna say.

"Who got my baby?" Auntie Frankie said walking from upstairs.

"Ummmm,"

"Don't fuckin *ummm* me. Where is my got damn child?"

"We don't know ma, somebody snatched her up."

"So, you mean to tell me my pregnant daughter has been taken?"

Before anyone could respond we heard a scream behind us. Looking behind me, I saw it'd came from A'yanni.

"Where is my TeTe? Is she coming back? Is she gonna die?" We were all in our own thoughts and forgot to make sure Yanni was out of earshot. She'd started having a panic attack and that wasn't good. "Da-da-daddy you you have to ge get my TeTe back. We lost Destiny, we can't lose my TeTe. Pleeeaaaasse Uncle Majik, you have to go find her!"

"Come on Lil bit, you know uncle don't like to see my lil gangster in training cry. Come on now calm down." Majik was good with kids and just like that she'd started calming down. "Have I ever let you down lil bit?"

"Well it was that one time when I was like five, I asked you for some skates and you never brought them. Then that one time when you didn't take me and Majesti to Magic Mountain when we asked. Oh, and that one time you made TeTe Nauti cry, but other than that no."

Everybody in the room laughed at the look on his face. It was just like Yanni to make us forget the pain we were feeling, even if it was just for a moment.

"Well I'll make it up to you big head ass lil girl."

"Just bring Majesti's annoying behind and TeTe home."

"Already," he replied

I guess it was Jaysun's turn to throw a fit cause without

warning he started punching the wall, leaving several holes behind.

"Yo dawg, yo oversized ass gonna pay for that shit too."

"Why we sitting up here laughing and joking like my damn girl and baby ain't out there missing?"

"If you had of paid more attention to your girl instead of slanging dick all over Atlanta, you'd probably know where your "girl" was at right now," Ahnais threw out there and I'm glad she said it.

"Ain't that the damn truth," I co-signed with her remark.

"Y'all might wanna know what the fuck y'all talking about before you open your mouth. Worry about your own shit."

"Aye my nigga, you better calm all that shit down. Watch how you talk to my fuckin girl," Majik told him calmly as he lit up his loud.

"Umm uncle Majik come here," Yanni said pulling him close to her so she could whisper, but of course we could still hear her. "Unc, you do know TeTe Nautica not your girl anymore. You messed that one up." She finished shaking her head.

He mushed her and walked away.

The guys had stepped out for a minute to hit the pavement but came back with no answers. Jaysun's eyes were bloodshot red and I knew exactly how he was feeling. Majesti wasn't my biological daughter, but I loved that girl like she'd came out of me. I know the hurt and pain he was feeling.

We were just sitting around waiting for Kwame and whoever else the guys called over to come. Auntie Frankie was going crazy waiting for some type of answer, phone call, or something that would give her answers to Amaris' whereabouts.

I was sitting down looking out in a daze when Majik took this as an opportunity to try talking to me again. I was mentally drained, and I seriously didn't have the energy to argue with him.

"You good shawty?"

"Nah, but I will be."

"Aye, I just wanna apologize to you again for the shit I said that day. On the real, I didn't mean it. I for real appreciate everything you've done for me with Majesti."

"Thank you, apology accepted."

"Can we maybe grab a bite to eat and talk once this shit over and done?"

"Right now, I don't think that's a good idea. I'm focused on getting myself together right now."

"I feel ya, shawty. But know I'm always here if you ever need me." He started walking away but turned back around. "Oh yeah, it's not safe for you to be at that house by yourself right now. Even though we got details on y'all, shit still ain't safe. Either you gonna have to stay back at the house with me or here with Ahnais and Draiven, you pick. It's not up for discussion though." He finished and walked off just as the doorbell rang.

I damn sure wasn't expecting him to say that. One thing I know for sure is that I wasn't going back to that house to stay with his ass. I'd stay here with Ahnais and sleep in between her and Draiven before I moved back in with Majik. Regardless of how short of a time it'd be, I'm not gonna do it. I refuse to give him the option to be able to try and break down my guard.

AHNAIS

If these muthafuckas don't boss up and find my got damn sister, they're gonna see a side of me they don't wanna see. I play about a lot of things but my fuckin sister ain't one of them.

The guys were waiting on Kwame and a few more people to come and help them make sense of this bullshit and find my sister. The doorbell rung and Draiven went to answer it. When he came back in the room the last person I expected to be with him came waltzing in.

"What the hell you doing at my house? Where is my fucking sister?"

I walked up to Solomon and slapped the shit of out him.

"I understand you're hurting and upset about Amaris, but don't ever put hands on me. I brought you in this world and you know the rest," he said in his Italian accent, sounding like an extra on Scarface.

"Muthafucka the day you touch my child will be the day you go meet yo punk ass pappy in hell."

"Aight look y'all need to chill out man for real. We ain't here for all this extra shit. This is the only person that can probably help us find Amaris. Y'all gonna have to check y'all emotions at the door and save it until we bring sis home. After that I don't care what the hell y'all do." Draiven said tryna call himself checking somebody.

"Who the hell you think you talking to? Nigga I'll clap your light skinned ass the fuck off," my mama told him.

I didn't even bother going in on him right now, but you better believe he was gonna have to see me about the way he was tryna handle me.

"Draiven why is he here? He's probably the one that had her kidnapped. You know psychopaths are known for doing shit like that."

"Shawty this ain't no damn movie, chill out!"

"Listen the longer y'all sit around here and play, the longer my daughter is out there not being found. I can go back and forth with you on another day sweetheart."

"You haven't earned the right to claim my daughter. If I'm not mistaken you didn't wanna have nothing to do with my kids. Niggas kill me wanna dip out on their responsibilities, but when they seeds grown or successful, they wanna come back around like they been the model parent."

"Aye Mama Frankie, y'all for real gonna have to save this

shit for the Ricky Lake, Judge Judy, Maury Povich or what the fuck ever. Amaris is out there pregnant with your grandchild and y'all doing this right now. Man come on for real," Majik spoke up and unfortunately he's right.

I'm super ashamed of how I allowed my anger for Solomon to get in the way of what's important in this moment.

"You're right bro, my bad."

Mama didn't say anything, and I didn't expect her to. We all sat down so we could figure this shit out. Yanni came in the living room and I could see the look on Solomon's face and it was one of admiration. I could see it in his eyes that he was feeling guilty about not knowing his granddaughter.

The moment Yanni was within arm's reach of him he stood up and actually started straightening out his tie and suit jacket like she was the Queen of England.

"Hello young lady and what's your name?"

"Ion know you like that to be giving you my information."

He laughed so hard shit it made the whole room join in.

"I'm sorry mi amore, I'm Solomon."

"Ohhh you're Solomon and what you want more of?" This girl is a trip. She don't ever get tired of talking. "I heard a lot about you, so you supposed to be my granddad huh?" She asked while walking around, looking him up and down while inspecting him head to toe.

"I hope it was all good things you heard mi amore."

"Uhh yeah no and what the heck is a mi amore? My name is Yanni. You gonna help bring my TeTe home though?"

"Yes, mi Yanni."

"You cool with me then pops. Oh yeah you owe me years' worth of birthday and Christmas gifts. I take cash and cards."

"YANNI!" we all yelled out.

"What?" She shrugged her shoulders. "He gotta catch up with my nana."

"Girl go back to your room and let them figure this mess out," I told her

"Aight pops, don't forget what I said." She bumped fist with him and walked away.

"No problem mi more."

She walked away mumbling about wanting to know why he kept calling her that. I wasn't about to explain cause that would've prolonged her going to her room.

Now that she was gone, and I made sure she wasn't eavesdropping, the guys got down to business.

"What exactly is his role in this?" I inquired.

"Let me start of by saying I apologize you girls were brought into this. I've recently taken over the head of our operation when my father passed away."

"May he rest in hell," my mama mumbled

"MAMA!"

"Don't come tryna check me Ahnais."

"No, I understand. Anyway, it's come to my attention my right-hand man didn't like how I planned to run things and he teamed up with my dumb nephew and my ungrateful son to have me taken out. It would be shameful on them to turn on me, so they planned to go after Marcelo. Of course, he's out, you guys were the next target. They wanted you to believe I was after you, so you'd take me out."

"You got a dumb ass team." I had to put my two cents out there. "Don't they know if the guys went after you, they'd kill everyone? Nobody leaves people to come back for revenge. The fuck?"

"You are indeed my child," he stated

"You don't even wanna go there with me."

"I apologize mi amore."

"And that mi amore shit only works on Frankie's ass."

"Bitch I'll punch you in yo throat. That Rico Suave shit don't work no more. I'm an old playa now."

"See what you left us with? I'm damaged!"

"Keep on playing with me Nais."

I waved her off and blew her a kiss and of course it wouldn't be her if she didn't shoot me a bird.

"So, where them muthafuckas at?" Lenyx asked. I guess whatever him and Selina was on the outs for was now repaired, cause she was all up under him.

"I haven't been able to get a location on them yet. I've been calling since Draiven called me."

"Kinda shit you running? You can't locate your got damn men."

"I guess the same shit you're running. You couldn't keep your daughter and sister in law safe. Don't come for me young man."

"Fuck you say nigga?" Majik jumped up in his face pissed off.

I mean Solomon did kinda have a point though.

"Young man I've told once and I'll tell you again, that shit don't put fear in my heart."

"Bruh chill the fuck out, we ain't here for that." Lenyx got in between the two as Solomon looked unfazed reaching inside his suite jacket pocket for his cigar. "Aye what's your people's address we gonna start there?" he looked at Selina and asked.

She looked real uncomfortable with everybody staring at her.

"Umm it's 2387 Jefferson Way, it's out there in Riverdale," she answers real nervous and I wanted to know what the hell was going on.

"What the hell going on Selina?" I asked

"Tell her!" Lenyx demanded.

"Well um so uh a couple of weeks ago I overheard my cousin Bianca talking to her boyfriend about trying to get at y'all. I just listened cause they were drunk just spilling tea. I never told her who I was seeing so I was able to listen without them shutting down."

"Ahhh hell naw. Don't tell me you on some bullshit? I done introduced you to my brother and brought you in to this family. Bitch you got me fucked up, I'll beat yo ass in here."

"No, I swear I'm not."

"Yo chill out sis, she straight. You know after the last bitch crossed me I wasn't gonna fall for the okey-doke. She been watched and checked out well before I hooked up with her the first time and every day since then. I promise y'all she cool."

"Bruh you better hope she is cause I ain't taking no more losses. I'll dead her ass in front of her peoples and make them fix me a full coarse me with her dead body sitting at the table," Majik spoke up.

"Got damn bro, I was just talking about beating her ass real quick. You on some Silence of the Lamb type shit."

I saw her get a little closer to him and he gave her a look.

"First of all, I said I wasn't involved in the shit and second, ain't nobody beating my ass," she stood up and said.

"Whew, girl bout time, you was about to have to go with that weak shit. For the record though, you'd get ya ass beat fucking with me."

"That's my child!" Mama and Solomon both said at the same time.

I looked at him with the *stop playing with me* look and he threw up his hands in surrender.

"Okay so what's next? If your cousin had something to do with my sister being taken I'm beating her ass and killing her, so pick out your black dress now."

"I want my one with her too if she took my TeTe."

"Why are you back downstairs? Got dammit you getting on my nerves today."

"I got hungry and thirsty, what you want me to do, starve?"

I looked at my mama and she immediately got up.

"I got her, I got her. You know that's what good grandparents do." She looked at Solomon throwing him major shade.

"You still want me, don't you?" With his thick accent he started taunting her. I see why she fell for him.

"Muthafucka I wish I would. You wouldn't get to even smell the top of my belly button again, let alone my pussy."

It's a good thing my damn child went ahead of her to the kitchen. This lady don't give a fuck what she says.

"Mama that's just nasty."

She shrugged her shoulders and kept on moving.

"We go to the cousin house to see if we can get anything out of her."

All the guys including Solomon got up and left. I was doing everything I could in order to not think about my sister. The sun had long ago set and Draiven still hadn't come home. No news was good news, so I was hopeful.

Nautica and Selina had been fell asleep, so I laid on the couch with my kindle reading this new author Hershe' Wrights called *The Young and the Reckless.* I'd read all of Nikki Brown's books, so I needed something new to read. I was trying to get through the first five chapters before I dozed off, but I'd felt my eyelids closing the moment I saw chapter two.

The next morning...
The fellas didn't get in until about three this morning and everybody just crashed here. I decided to get up and fix breakfast for everyone since I knew they'd been out all night looking for Amaris.

I was just about finish with setting everything out on the table when the doorbell rang. It's was only ten a.m. so I had no idea who could be at our house this damn early. I tied my robe and made my way to the door. Before I could even turn the doorknob,

Solomon came out of nowhere stopping me. I didn't even know he was here too.

"Don't open the door. We don't know who could be out there."

"You don't tell me what to do, if you hadn't noticed I'm grown. Your time has expired."

"Listen you can be mad all you want to, but while you're in my presence I'll continue to make sure you're safe."

"Ahnais chill the fuck out man, I'm too tired for your shit this morning. This man tryna keep your ass alive. Deal with your other shit another day."

He shoved me out the way to answer the door.

"Who are you and what the fuck you doing at my house so early bruh?"

"I'm looking for Ahnais Davenport."

"Fuck you need wit my girl?"

"I'm Ahnais, how can I help you officer."

"Ahnais Davenport, you've been served."

He handed me a large envelope and walked away. I was so confused as to why I was being served.

Reading the papers tears immediately fell down my cheeks.

"Babe what's wrong? What you crying for?"

"My my baby. Somebody is trying to take my baby!"

I was crying so loud I damn near woke up the whole damn house. Majik, Nautica, and my mama made their way towards me.

"Girl what are you talking about?"

My mama snatched the papers out of my hand. She started reading them over and I could see her getting pissed.

"Who the fuck is Dramond Gordon and why would he be suing you for joint custody?"

"Umm auntie Dramond is Draego's real name," Nautica spoke up.

"Yooooo this nigga about to die a slow ass death. Stop that fucking crying man. Ain't nobody bout to take my daughter. His bitch ass ain't gonna live long enough to see that court date."

I did the best I could trying to calm down, but all I could think about was those papers. If I lost my baby, I didn't know what I would do. I knew he knew she looked familiar to him cause unfortunately she favored his rapist ass so much.

We all sat down to eat the breakfast I made but I couldn't take not one bite. I just kept looking at my daughter and praying.

Lord please don't take my daughter!!

COCO

I don't know how much longer I'll be able to take this bullshit. Draego's been treating me like shit since we've been out here. Worse than what he'd been treating me before. My daughter is fucking miserable and I know it's all my got damn fault.

The more Majesti ask for her daddy the more he hits her. I didn't care at this point if Majik killed me, I just wanted my baby safe. I was determined to find a way to get in contact with her daddy.

I knew if Majik didn't get me Draego would eventually do it, so either way I was gonna meet my damn maker.

What scared me the most is when his so-called friends brought in a pregnant woman and after being nosey I saw it was Amaris. Why in the hell he got involved with these crazy ass people was beyond me.

"CoCo! Coco go fix that bitch something to eat! I don't need her ass dying just yet. I want them muthafuckas to watch me kill her ass."

"She ain't gonna eat nothing from me Draego," I said rolling my eyes.

I don't know what the hell I even did that for. I knew what was coming next. He punched me in my eye and I dropped straight to the floor. He squatted down to my level and lifted my head up by my hair.

"I think you like getting your ass beat. I don't know why you can't just shut the fuck up and do as I say. Now get your stupid ass up and fix that bitch something to eat."

My eye was already swelling up and I really don't know how his dumb ass expected me to be able to see enough to get in this kitchen. But of course, he didn't at all think about that.

Looking in the fridge I searched for the quickest thing I could cook up. I didn't like not being able to keep my eyes on Majesti. Ever since the day I heard Draego tell them guys that he'd raped Ahnais a long time ago and had a plan to ruffle her feathers with Yanni, I didn't want him alone with her.

I found some pork chops that needed to be used before they went bad. I seasoned them real good and fried them up. Opening up a can of green beans, I made them like they were made from scratch with a pot of buttered rice. After about an hour the food was finally done. I fixed that devil a plate first cause I wasn't in the mood for another knock down fight with him. Once I made sure he was good, I fixed three other plates and took two to Majesti's room.

"Here Maj, I cooked something to eat." I couldn't bear to see the sad and depressing look in her eyes. It killed my soul every time.

I wish I would have realized in the beginning that getting revenge on her father was more important than her happiness. I was too stupid to get it.

"Do you love me at all?" she looked up asking me. Her question threw me off because it came out of nowhere.

"Yes, I love you, why would you even ask me that?"

"You've never showed me love. You never tried to do mother daughter stuff with me like Nauti use to. Every time you got me, you took me right back to my daddy. Now I don't even have my daddy cause you took me away from him. I don't have anybody to love me. I just want my daddy."

"Majesti I'm sorry. I know I'll probably never get to make it up to you, but I'm sorry. I do love you but honestly, I didn't know how to be a mother to you. I was never shown love from my mama, so I didn't know how to give it to you."

She looked at me and nodded her head like she understood. I jumped up and looked out the door, I needed to make sure Draego wasn't somewhere listening to our conversation and lurking. "I'm gonna get you home to your daddy Majesti, I promise you I am."

For the first time since we've been here she smiled at me. Wrapping her little arms around my neck, she squeezed with all her might and I knew I was gonna have to do the right thing.

"Thank you, mama. I love you and I'm sorry grandma was mean to you."

"Thank you chipmunk and you're welcome. I'm going to feed your auntie you wanna walk down there with me?"

She shook her head and we made our way to the basement. Once I grabbed her plate I headed downstairs.

"TeTe guess what mama said she was gonna make sure daddy comes to get us."

I looked at Amaris and knew she wanted to say something smart, but for the sake of Majesti she didn't.

"Is that right baby girl?"

"Yep aren't you happy TeTe?"

I knew she didn't believe it and didn't want to get her hopes up. She rubbed her pregnant belly and tried to discreetly wipe the tears from her eyes. I saw it, so I know my daughter saw it.

"Well that's good Maji."

"Don't cry TeTe we're gonna make it home. We brought you some food."

Any other time she would not eat, it seems like the only time she did is when she saw Majesti.

"Y'all get the fuck back up here!" Draego yelled from the top of the basement steps.

"I'm gonna get them here, just hang tight." She rolled her eyes but shook her head.

"Love you TeTe."

"Love you more buttercup."

I grabbed her hand, so she didn't fall going up the stairs and no sooner than we made it to him he slapped me across my face.

"Stop it. Stop hitting my mommy!" Majesti cried out. She never said anything when he hit me, so I was shocked.

He stopped hitting me and in one quick swift motion he took his belt off with one hand and whacked her across the back. She screamed out and he turned it on me. After hitting me several times all over my body he stopped suddenly.

"CoCo don't make me have to kill you and that lil bitch. You better not be up to nothing."

His phone rung and he walked away to answer it. I had to pick Majesti up even though I could barely move myself.

I overheard him talking to the guys that kidnapped Amaris I knew they were coming over soon. I had go get my plan in motion. I quickly made my way to Majesti's room to put her in bed.

"I'm so sorry sweetie, I'mma get your daddy here tonight, just hold tight okay?"

I kissed her forehead and left out.

Saying a quick prayer, it's now or never.

Lord please protect my daughter. Forgive me for all my wrongdoings. I know I don't deserve your forgiveness, but please help me get Majesti back with her daddy. Amen!

Well here we go!

MAJIK

I don't know why muthafuckas continue to try my patience. I ain't got none left so everybody was about to got damn get it. The day my daughter was taken was the day I stopped giving a fuck about everything. Anybody who looked like they wanted smoke, I laid them the fuck down. I damn near dismantled my whole muthafuckin team from killing they ass. I wasn't taking no shit from nobody. We'd be beating the streets day in and day out looking for Majesti and my sis. I was betting money that wherever one was the other was there or not too far.

I don't think that nigga Jaysun would be able to survive another loss. Being that he'd just lost Destiny not too long ago, I'm almost certain that if he lost another baby on top of losing his girl, this nigga was gonna have to be committed. We bout came to blows a few times, but I had to understand what that man was going through.

We got the address to Selina's cousin Bianca's house and went to pay her lil ass a visit the other night. She wasn't there the first time we went, but we stayed around a few hours and got lucky the next go around. She wanted to play that ride or die tough girl role, but today was the day I broke her from that shit. After I get her to spill the beans, I'mma keep her alive long enough to show her why she should never put her all into a simp ass nigga. I bet you that clown ass fool wouldn't hesitate to throw her goofy ass up under the bus. These musty ass bitches gonna learn though.

One thing I know, I don't have to worry about Majesti or Yanni growing up being stupid for a nigga. We been teaching them from birth about having the right man's back.

Me and my niggas had just made it to the warehouse and it was time to get some got damn answers. I didn't know who I wanted to start with Kaycie or Bianca, so I was gonna use them both at the same time.

"Nigga I swear if this bitch on some bullshit today, I might do this hoe dirty on the spot!" Jaysun was too hyped up and I knew it wouldn't be a good idea for him to question Bianca.

If he came off the top being aggressive, she wasn't gonna be willing to help us at all. I peeped just from being around her those few minutes, she had to feel like she was needed.

"Man look, you not in the right frame of mind to handle this bitch right now. I know you want to get your girl back, but I also want to get my daughter back. We can't afford for nothing to go wrong."

"Man fuck all that, that hoe better talk or else!"

"Jaysun, for real dawg you need to chill the fuck out. This shit gonna be worth it, trust me." Draiven interjected. "I wanna find these fools too. This bitch nigga raped my girl, got her pregnant, and then gonna come back and try to get custody like he didn't do that fuck shit. Yeah I need to get my hands on him and this skank bitch may be our only lead right now."

"Yeah aight, whatever!"

See that's that hoe behavior I been talking about. His ass better get that shit under control and quick. I ain't with that bullshit.

I had thought about having Draiven call up Solomon to have him sit in on this little meeting, but I changed my mind. Even though that nigga may not be involved this time, that don't mean he won't ever come after us. I didn't need him knowing too much about our operation and where some our spots was at. Too many people knowing your business was always bad for business.

While Lenyx and Draiven went to the back to get them hoes, I took a quick moment to send Nautica a text. She was adamant on not coming to stay at the house with me and I couldn't do shit but respect it. I know I said some foul shit and I couldn't do nothing but hope one day she would forgive me and move forward. Hopefully when she moved forward, it was with me.

Me: Sup shawty you good?

Wifey: Yeah why you ask that?

Me: No reason ma, just checking. I'mma be that way in a lil bit did you need anything?

Wifey: Nah not really and you don't have to keep tryna be nice to me.

I've known her long enough to know when she says not really that she really did want something but was just too damn stubborn to admit it and tell me what it was she wanted. She was trying her best to keep that lil guard up.

Me: girl stop tripping, what the hell do you need? You forgot I know you, I know when yo stubborn ass really want something.

Wifey: Whatever Majik

Me: Shawty for real you irritating the fuck outta me. What the hell you need?

Wifey: I don't care about you bein irritated, nigga you texted me. ANYWAYYYY! I need some tampons, a bag of snickers minis, and some size C batteries. Can you also please go to Taco Bell and get me something to eat?

I know her cycle was probably due to come on soon. She always had crazy cravings right before she came on. I was starting to regret asking her if she needed anything. We'd had them a vacation time off from work and made them stay in the house until this shit was over so, I wasn't gonna have a choice but to get all this bullshit.

Me: damn man, send me what your greedy ass wants. I'll be done with what I'm doing in about an hour and I'll be headed that way.

Wifey: Whatever, get me three steak Chalupas no sour cream, nacho fries, a watermelon freeze, and an order of

Cinnabon delights twelve pack. Make sure you get me a lot of mild sauce.

Me: aight, love you shawty.

I sent that last message just as them hoes was being thrown in the room. I knew she wasn't gonna respond, but it was fun as hell fucking with her.

It was time to get this damn show on the road.

"Aight listen I hope you bitches was able to get acquainted. Kaycie, you've known us for a while am I right?"

"Ye, yeah."

"So, you know I'm not into playing games." Once she shook her head, I continued on with what I needed her to hear. "Call that bitch and see if you can get her to answer."

I've had that hoe's phone ever since we snatched her up and she hadn't gotten not one call from CoCo. I was on standby waiting. I dialed the number, putting it on speaker as it rung. After it rung several times there was no answer as it was sent to voicemail.

"Kaycie you've had a lot of time to think about this, did she say anything that you can think of that would tell us where she might be at?"

"No Majik I swear, I would have told you when you first asked. She wouldn't tell me where they were at."

"Did you hear my daughter around?"

"No, I didn't but I know she is for sure with her."

"I don't recall if I asked you this or not, but did you know she was planning on running off with my daughter?"

She immediately started crying and shaking. Just from her

reaction alone, I knew she'd known. She knew I was a good ass father so for her to have been okay with that shit pissed me off on so many fucking levels.

Before she could give me an explanation I pulled out my strap and shot her ass in the leg. I didn't want her dead just yet. I was gonna make CoCo watch me dismember her body limb by limb.

"Ahhhhhhhh Majik pleasssee. I don't know anything! Please don't killl me!"

This bitch sitting next to her was starting to realize that this shit wasn't a game. She was rocking back and forth biting her lip.

Draiven stepped up in front of Bianca and Len stepped to the side of her.

"Do you know who I am Ms. Bianca?" Lenyx asked her kneeling down.

"No, am I supposed to?"

"You might as well drop that tough girl shit bitch. I see the tremble all up and through ya body," Draiven told her ass with the quickness.

"Let me introduce myself, I'm Lenyx. You might know my girl Selina." Her eyes got bucked as hell. "I have a few questions for you. Did you use my girl, so you and your bitch ass boyfriend could get close to us?"

"No, I didn't know, but honestly if I did I probably would have."

""Preciate your honesty shawty. Where is your punk ass nigga at though?"

"I don't know."

"So, we back on this Ms. Bianca? I thought we'd all became friends!"

"Listen hoe!" Draiven pulled out this Glock, grabbed her ponytail pulling her head, and put it right on her temple. "Because of your bitch ass nigga and his Power Ranger crew, my girl been crying every day cause her sister gone and the nigga that raped her is a part of it. On top of that, that nigga tryna take my baby, not to mention he beat on my sister for years. So, excuse me if I'm not in the mood to deal with you pretending to play stupid. I will shoot you in every part of your body and make sure you stay alive to feel it. Stop playing with me." He shot her in her left foot and then shot her ass again in her right leg.

He meant he wasn't playing any games.

"Ahh fucckkkkkk! I'm telling you the damn truth I don't know!"

"Shawty we can do this all day every day. So, until you give us something we can use, we gonna do this shit every got damn day." I told her, making sure she understood every word I was saying.

The hood doctor came in and doctored them both up. I meant what I said, I would do this daily until they cooperated.

We made sure them broads was treated and straight before leaving them with their thoughts and wounds.

Maybe sitting there for a few hours would put some fire under their ass.

I was in Walmart with Jaysun searching hard for these got damn tampons. I forgot which kind she used and I damn sure wasn't about to ask, she would start talking shit about me forgetting. After searching through a few more brands I got the two I'd seen her use and headed for the candy isle. I wasn't sure if she had something for her cramps for whenever she does come on, so I also grabbed some aspirin and a heating pad just in case.

Looking at Bruh I could tell he had some major shit on his mind.

"Dawg what the fuck going on with you? You been with that bullshit."

I know he was worried about his girl, but this was some other shit.

He looked around and rubbed his hand down his head as he sighed.

"I fucked up man, I fucked up bad."

"Spill it!"

"Aight so look, a nigga was depressed when I found out Maris was pregnant, I didn't want her to have the baby. I was for real scared of losing them. I was drinking hard one night at the strip club and let one of them bitches top me off."

"NIGAAAAA!" I said shaking my head

"The bitch thought I was gonna cuff her ass and been fucking with Amaris. I think that's why she tried to get away."

"Dawg you gotta handle that shit before we get her back."

"What do I do man?"

"Kill the bitch!" I shrugged my shoulder and made my way to the checkout counter.

I took my ass to Taco Bell ordered all this shit and head to Draiven's house. I knew this nigga could handle that shit himself but wasn't gonna let him go alone. I handed Nautica her shit and told her I'd be right back. Her ugly ass rolled her eyes, but I didn't give no fucks bout that shit. She was gonna have to see me as much as I wanted her to.

Grabbing all the fellas, we headed back out. We designated Bruh's house as the main spot for the moment. It was ducked off and big enough.

"Fuck we going man? I was just about to get me some muthafuckin pussy!" Len fussed

"Word!" Draiven said agreeing.

"This nigga done got his dick in trouble so we going to handle this shit before we get sis back."

I had his dumb dick ass explain what the fuck he'd gotten himself into while heading to the hoe crib. It was still light out, so I didn't need our faces to be the seen at her spot on some suspect shit. I had a plan that I knew would work.

Back at the house...

We were all sitting around waiting for Solomon to get here. I still didn't trust his ass, but hey who am I. That's they peoples, so I wasn't in it. Until he did some shady shit, I was staying out their family drama.

"I'm about to fix something to eat, y'all want something?" Sis asked

"Hellz yeahhh." That shit came right on time cause a nigga was hungry as fuck.

Out of nowhere somebody started banging on the door and

we all jumped up pulling out our guns and shit. You never know who the hell was out there.

Draiven looked on the camera and noticed in was Kwame. That was strange cause I don't recall nobody saying he was coming by.

Soon as he opened the door I pointed my shit at his head.

"Fuck you doing popping up nigga?"

"Put that shit up nigga, I'm bout to make your day. So, check this out," he said hyped as fuck pulling out his laptop. "I had it setup to alert me if your daughter's phone ever came back on. Nigga I got a hit." This muthafucka was bouncing all around, making me nervous and shit.

He was working to get us a location when my phone rung. I was so busy talking shit, I didn't bother looking at the caller I.D.

"What up, who this?"

"Daddy. Daddy it's me."

"Majesti, hey baby girl. Where you at? Tell daddy where you at so I can come get you." I could barely get the words out. Between Nautica all up in my face tryna take my phone and the tears threatening to fall out my eyes, I couldn't focus.

"Daddy you gotta hurry up and come now."

"Okay baby daddy is coming. Are you okay? They didn't hurt you, did they?"

Before she could answer Nautica managed to snatch the phone.

"Majesti are you okay baby? We're coming I promise."

"Nauti! I missed you. I gotta go. I hear somebody coming."

"Got it!" Kwame yelled.

That's all I needed to hear.

"Majesti if you can turn the phone on vibrate like I showed you, but don't turn it off. Hide it somewhere where only you know where it is. I'm coming now!"

"Okay daddy but hurry up!"

"I gotcha pumpkin."

I didn't wanna ask her if Amaris was with her because if she wasn't, I didn't need her knowing she was missing.

These muthafuckas done fucked up. They wanted my attention now they got it. I was about to let these bitch ass niggas feel the magic.

"Strap up niggas, let's go get Amaris and my baby girl!

To Be Continued…..

CPSIA information can be obtained
at www.ICGtesting.com
Printed in the USA
LVHW031814230419
615253LV00002B/264